Imaginative, exciting! A Hogwarts for secret agents. *Domino 29* will knock you over!

—Bestselling author Andrew Gross

Move over, James Bond: there's a new kid in town and he's way cooler. In *Domino 29*, author Axel Avian introduces us to Agent Colt Shore, a young, globetrotting secret agent who gets swept into an adventure he—and every reader—will not soon forget. Axel Avian has crafted a masterpiece of high stakes, fast action and intriguing characters. It's a story that will have readers racing ~~through~~ trying in vain to catch their ~~thr~~illing must-read!

—Robert Liparulo, author of the *~~Dre~~amhouse Kings* and *The 13th Tribe*

AGENT COLT SHORE

DOMINO
29

AGENT COLT SHORE

DOMINO
29

by
Axel Avian

JF AUI

CONTENTS

This story is true.
The names and identities have been
changed to protect active assignments.
FALCON's agents of change are probably in your town.
Possibly eating cashew chicken.
For more information,
go to www.ColtShore.com

For Joey

Bravest of us all.

And always in our hearts.

AGENT COLT SHORE

DOMINO
29

PROLOGUE

I'M LOCKED IN a small chapel, an oratory, in a Gothic castle. I'm badly hurt. With me are eleven girls, dressed in color-splashed tunics, pants, and *chadors*. They're terrified. We have three minutes. Three minutes to escape, or be captured.

A week ago, I was a normal kid. Not a secret agent at all.

As far as I can tell, it was one of those domino chain reactions. You've probably seen the videos where people set up thousands of dominos in a pattern, then push the first one and watch them all go. But did you know that, with dominos, a different kind of chain reaction is possible? That a domino the size of a tiny piece of gum can knock over the next one that's one and a half times larger, and so on, until with twenty-nine dominos, you've started with the one the size of gum and are knocking over one the size of the Empire State Building?

Has your life ever spiraled out of control like that? Where if you had changed just one thing, one tiny thing, none of the rest of it would have happened?

Never mind one thing leading to the next that is crazier, to the next, crazier yet—and before you know it, you're in a huge castle in the Alps, injured, chased by men with guns, trying to save twelve lives.

For me, it all started because I got a pair of drumsticks out of my backpack.

CHAPTER ONE

Everything Changes

HERE'S THE THING: it's tough having an older brother who's a hero. It's even tougher when he's dead, because as often as you screw up, he's never going to screw up again. He's perfect. He's also frozen in time at twenty-two, forever handsome—winning smile, great teeth, sparkle in his eye. I know because there's a photo of him that's the first thing you see when you walk in the front door. It's why I came in through the kitchen.

All my life, I'd heard what a great tragedy it is that he's gone. Left unsaid was what a letdown it is that I remain instead. Fifteen and awkward and unfinished.

His name was Dix, short for Dixon, and he died before I was born. I was the consolation prize. By the time I came along, my parents were older. Not only older, but also slightly used up. As if they'd spent all their energy on their only son, and when their second only son came along, they had to go to the reserve energy tanks, which didn't work quite as well. I slept in the bedroom that had been his, grew up in the same town, went to the same special save-the-world school, even had some of the same teachers, whom I imagined looked at me with sympathy rather than admiration. I was the also-ran.

Or that's what I thought until my Uncle Don came to dinner that September Monday at our cream-colored brick home on Brent Hill in Springfield, Missouri. We had herbed chicken and rutabagas. He was a favorite uncle, never married, constantly in good humor. He was always glad to see me, always called me "Colt my boy," as if "my boy" was my middle name.

They were at the dinner table having decaf coffee and angel food cake when I asked to be excused. I decided to practice my drums before finishing my homework, because Uncle Don was a music fan back from when they actually called it "rock 'n' roll." So I went to my room, cranked up the music, and sat down behind my

Ludwigs to finish working out the drum part to a new song by a band I liked. I'd been through it once but I wanted a different sound. Then I remembered I had some new jazz drumsticks in my backpack.

I let the band continue to wail while I headed out to the front hall to fetch them.

Domino one.

I wasn't sneaking, or being especially quiet. I was still digging the drumsticks out of my backpack when I heard Uncle Don say, "He's getting pretty good on those drums. He might be good enough to play in a professional band. Has he said what he'd like to be? A professional drummer, or does he show any of his dad's interest in being a secret agent?"

This stopped me in my tracks. My dad had never been an agent. He was an engineer.

"No," said Mom, "thank the Lord."

A pause. Then Uncle Don said, "Don't you sometimes wish his parents could see him? I think they'd be so proud."

There was dead air. Then Mom said, pointedly, "We've discussed this."

It was right about then that the hall tilted. I had to put my hand out to the wall to steady myself. After a minute of gulping breath, I lurched back to my bedroom.

So my parents weren't my parents.

Lucy and Victor Shore weren't actually my parents.

The information was such a shock that I didn't know what to do. I didn't know which way to turn.

The next day was pretty much lost to me. I went to school; I came home. I stared straight ahead most of the time. Lucy and Victor tried to talk to me, but I wasn't in the mood. They didn't know why and I wasn't about to tell them. I was mad that the people I had trusted most in the world had lied to me. My whole life.

At school that day, I did tell my best friend, Luke, because he had the good sense to ask me in private, and "Turns out Lucy and Victor aren't my parents" sounded very dramatic when spat out at the locker bank. Luke was way impressed, gave me a "whoa" look, and said, "So who are your parents?"

Wow. I hadn't gotten there yet.

All through my next classes, I pondered. All I knew for sure was that my biological father was an agent. Did they say my mother was also? I couldn't remember.

Here were my leading theories: my parents were the top agents in the world, deep undercover in the former Soviet Union, so they couldn't raise me.

Or, my father was an agent and my mother was

a civilian and they kidnapped me to be raised as a SuperBot agent.

Or, my parents were the top agents, ever, and they got killed. So FALCON, the international organization that runs my school, gave me to Lucy and Victor because raising heroes was their specialty. Except it sounded like my parents were alive and *could* come see me and be proud, but Lucy and Victor "had discussed this."

Then I thought of all the meat and potatoes they served, and how boring my life really was, and how Victor and Lucy seemingly *didn't* want me to be an agent. But maybe that was reverse psychology.

The next thing I consciously remember was going to school on Wednesday. I've lived in Springfield, Missouri, all my life, but I'm pretty sure nobody there even realizes our school exists. It's a training academy for an organization called the Free Alliance for the Lasting Cooperation of Nations, or FALCON. It's an organization that isn't affiliated with any government, but works quietly to solve some of the world's problems.

The high school is sort of a weird combination of secret-agent training and think tank. Most of the students don't go active—become field agents. Most of us become the brains behind the operations. We spend so much of the day studying history and current events to figure out why things happen the way they do and what, if anything, can be done about it, that among ourselves we usually refer to the school as "Why? High." Unlike regular high schools whose students adore the captain of the football team or the head cheerleader, our "firsts among equals" are the older students, like Jonathan Kryder, who are already active field agents, called on at times to go out to try to change the world.

The main building is almost all glass and chrome, so there's a lot of light. But it's one-way glass, so you can't see inside. There's also some sort of dome projection thing happening, so if you fly over it in a plane, it looks like the place is forested. Pretty cool.

By your junior year, you've usually chosen a track that reflects your personal interests. Mine is the countries that border the Mediterranean. Usually, when my life isn't falling apart, I do find that stuff really interesting.

I was sitting in the café at one of the small circular tables with Luke. I'd gone to the sushi bar but had no interest in anything on my plate. Luke was sitting next to me, not talking. That's how good of a friend he was.

Jonathan Kryder, also known as Jonny "Baad" Kryder (which I'm told was a nickname given him by a girlfriend—the nickname stuck, unlike the relationship), was sitting two tables away with a couple other kids from the agent track, but he wasn't talking much to them. Why should he? They weren't active yet and he was too school for cool. Whereas I wasn't talking because I wasn't a person who actually existed. Jonny wore his dark brown hair long. Today he had it pulled back in a ponytail; his flashing brown eyes looked like he knew deep secrets the rest of us would never understand.

I played with my sushi and looked up toward the windows, catching several other tables in my side vision. Second table over. Yes. She was looking at me like she was hoping to catch my eye.

Why would she be doing this? Why would Malin James be looking at me?

Malin James is very pretty, not cheerleader gorgeous or anything, but very pretty, with long blondish-brown hair and a body that was made for short skirts and sweaters. Which she seldom wore. She was quiet and kind instead of out there and popular. Way out of my league. As in, don't-even-try-it out of my league.

So why was she looking at me now? Could she tell I was no longer who I thought I was? If I wasn't Colt Shore, I was nobody. Why would they let a nobody into this school, anyhow?

Okay, enough already. This was too much moaning even for me.

"I have to do something. I have to find out who my parents are," I said to Luke.

"It's about time," he said. "You aren't a good moper. Too much drama. So, what are you going to do?"

"Where would the information be? My birth certificate. But who knows where that is?"

"Also, maybe your school records."

Luke and I both thought for a moment. The days of distracting the counselor so you could pull out your manila folder were long past. In fact, the CIA couldn't break into the FALCON computer system—though not for lack of trying.

"You know what would list them for sure?" I posited. "My medical records."

"Yeah, for sure," he responded. "So, how do you get those?"

"I'm suddenly not feeling very well," I said.

"So, what's the plan?"

I made it up as I was speaking it. "I'll go to the medical office, say I'm having a relapse of something I had last winter, and once my file has been pulled up online, you create a distraction in the hall. Just long enough that I can look."

Luke looked uncomfortable. "What would I do?"

"Fall down. Yell like you broke your ankle or something."

"I don't know . . ."

"How hard is this? You hurt your ankle. Then I come out of the office saying I'm feeling better, and we both go about our days."

He still looked dubious, but he said he'd try.

"You'll do it? Or you'll try?"

"I'll do it."

I stood up and grabbed my side. It was obvious Luke couldn't have too much time to think about this. I lurched out of the café toward the medical wing.

Domino two.

The aide wasn't at her desk. I walked gingerly back to the office of Nurse Bennett, the school's medical officer. Thankfully, no other students were in there. We don't have too many posers at Why? High.

"I think something's wrong," I gasped. "I think it's that thing . . . that thing I got last winter."

"What thing, Colt?" he asked. He was a young man, thirty maybe, with his hair shaved short. He was about my height. Today he wore a polo shirt and chinos.

"You know, you know," I said, clutching my side and

sliding into the chair by the wall. "Why I was out in November."

That specific was all he needed to touch the MediPad on the wall, and say, "Colton Shore."

My file came up. He flipped a screen or two before I could catch Luke's eye, where he stood out in the hall. He walked back out of sight, then turned around at a run, slipped, and slid just past the hall door. "Yaow!" he screeched.

Nurse Bennett didn't move. "Yeoww!" Luke howled again.

"Do you need help?" said a female voice, likely a helpful student in the hall.

"Help!" Luke yelled.

Nurse Bennett pulled himself away from my file, gave me an apologetic look, and headed into the hall.

I didn't even wait for him to pass the doorway. I jumped up and scrolled easily back to the "personal" page in my medical records. It occurred to me then that they might say nothing but that Lucy and Victor Shore were my parents, and all this would be for nothing.

Instead: page one. Name: Colton Timothy Shore.

Parents: Father:

And there it was. The name.

That's when the plan fell apart. I didn't get the

needed information and saunter out to the hallway to relieve Luke from his playacting.

I fell backward onto the chair, my mouth open.

I was still sitting there in shock when Nurse Bennett came back in to see me.

"What is it, Colt? What's wrong?" he asked.

There was only one thing wrong.

Dix wasn't my hero brother.

Dix was my dad.

CHAPTER TWO

Agent Coltrane

VICTOR CAME TO pick me up. Apparently, he'd been alerted to the situation by Nurse Bennett. The car ride home was silent.

Lucy was in the hall, waiting for us.

"So, what's the deal?" I asked. "Are you my grandparents?"

"Yes," said Lucy, and she came over to put her arms around me. I pulled away, went to my room, and locked the door.

I stayed in my room all evening. When Lucy and Victor left for work Thursday morning, I finally came out and ate about twelve Hot Pockets. While I did, Luke texted me, "You have to come in. Crawley is interviewing Greek finance minister."

Greece, of course, was a country bordering the Mediterranean. Still, nope.

Then: "Come in tomorrow. Amber Coltrane here."

Nope.

Until, of course, it was the next morning and Victor and Lucy left for work and I was really, really bored. Amber Coltrane had to be better than *Pawn Stars*. Especially reruns.

Amber Coltrane was one of FALCON's top agents. Agents like her are the reason every one of us was in this school. She was smart, funny, and completely down to earth. How to impress her? Kids in New York at the School of Performing Arts can show off their skills by singing. But how do you show off reasoning skills?

Agent Coltrane joined us in Precision Dance. It's a mixed class—boys and girls—designed to keep us in shape and sharpen our reflexes. We were learning a new routine, and she fell in with us. We all messed up; we all laughed a lot—especially her.

Later in the day, Agent Coltrane also visited my D-level class on the Mediterranean countries. There are only eight of us in the class, since it's an in-depth specialization. Unlike the physical training gear she'd worn in dance, she now wore black trousers and a square-cut jacket with a sapphire-blue blouse. Agent Coltrane's hair was golden blonde and shoulder length. She was in good shape.

She listened carefully to the discussion of that day's current events in Athens and to what historic and recent factors had caused them. She asked thoughtful questions, causing each of us to dig deeper and think about things in different ways. Her green eyes lit fire when someone came up with a new line of thought; she'd hold on to it and let you explore.

The fact that she liked one of my theories and spent nearly ten minutes building on it with me and the others in the class was enough to cause me to temporarily leave all the annoyances of my life behind.

I was in my next class when a runner came with a note saying Agent Coltrane wanted to speak with me in the office.

It felt like, somehow, I was expecting this.

As I walked the glass halls, I tried to keep my thoughts from revving out of control. What could she possibly want with me? I was on a T track—gathering and interpreting data that would be helpful to the agents out in the world. What if she'd seen something different in me? If she asked me to go active, what would I say? Could I handle it? Would I want to handle it?

I took a deep breath and pushed through the office door.

Inside the main office, Agent Dulaine, my track mentor, and Commandant Esper, head of the school, both waited for me. Agent Dulaine buzzed me in. "Sir," I said to him as I passed. He and the office assistants stopped their chatter and turned to watch me. Agent Dulaine had plentiful, dark hair and the build of a former quarterback. He usually looked semiamused and totally in control. Now he looked nervous, like he thought I might screw up and somehow bring dishonor to his students—in fact, to anyone whose last name started with *S* through *Z*.

"This way." Commandant Esper pressed her thumbprint on the scanner pad to open the gate in the back of the office. She had black hair pulled back in a large barrette, and she wore a fitted red dress. We were all pretty much in awe of her.

Together we walked back past the meeting rooms where mentors and students met, and past a Level 2 security meeting room. We came to the end of the hall. She flipped up the light switch and punched in another fingerprint and a quick series of numbers. The whole wall slid back to reveal more hall. We walked through. I'd never been back here. Had no idea it existed. Maybe, in case of nuclear holocaust, it's where all the office workers would survive until they had to resort to cannibalism. I wondered if there was a hot plate.

Maybe Agent Dulaine had reason to worry. Or maybe I was thinking silly things to keep from getting unbearably nervous.

We came to another dead end, this one lined with live trees in pots and hanging baskets of ivy. Another hidden keypad; a print from a different finger, and more numbers. One of the trees, and the wall behind it, slid open to reveal a door.

The commandant knocked on it. Within a minute, it slid open. Amber Coltrane stood there smiling warmly. "Thank you so much, Cheryl," she said, then stepped aside and I walked past. The door panel slid shut behind me.

"Sorry about all this," she said. "Everyone assumes I spend my days in Class 5 Security."

We now stood in a small, glassed room filled with flowers and plants. A small waterfall spilled into a pool against the back wall.

I tried not to let my mouth fall open at the sight of the jungle room. She motioned me to a small sofa; I did my best to walk normally across the room and sat. She sat in a comfortable-looking gray chair across from me.

"We haven't been officially introduced," she said. "Amber Coltrane."

"Colton. Shore."

She shook my hand. "It's very nice to see you, Colt," she said, and she looked at me as if she meant it. "In fact, it's why I came. Your grandparents told me you'd recently found out some new information about Dix, and I asked to talk to you. You see, he was my partner. We worked together for two years. There are things you should know about him—things I'd like you to know."

Whoa. My breath caught in my throat, causing me to have trouble breathing. This meeting had suddenly gone from being professional to being intensely personal.

Within the last five days, my understanding of the world had cracked wide open. I was still numb, still couldn't grasp what had happened. But she knew. She knew that Victor and Lucy were my grandparents. And she'd known my bro—my dad. She'd been his partner. Agents are trained to rely heavily on their partners. They trust each other with their lives. She'd known my dad.

"I don't know what you've heard about Dix, or what ideas you've formed about him. You would have really liked him. And he would have been crazy about you.

You've got his eyes—and his smile. You're so like him, it's kind of spooky."

She looked softer, somehow, than she had during the day. Like she was less of an agent and more of a person. This weirded me out even further.

"And he had these dimples. I might have only been sixteen, but it wasn't hard to notice the effect he had on women—including other agents. But Dix was seriously involved with Callie Anderson, and I never saw him cheat on her, or even lead anyone else on. You'll probably want to talk with her . . . when you're ready."

Agent Coltrane cleared her throat and sat forward on her chair.

"I'm here because I wanted to tell you about . . . about the day he died. It's something I think you should know, that's all. Dix died saving my life."

CHAPTER THREE

What Happened in Spain

AGENT COLTRANE SIGHED and sat back. Obviously, this was not an easy story for her to tell. I had no idea how to feel. So I let all the emotions wash over me without landing on one.

"I became a field agent when I was twelve, because my dad was one, and they needed someone to send in where adults wouldn't be welcomed. Dix became my partner when I was fourteen and he was twenty. It must have taken incredible patience for him to put up with me, but he never complained—in my hearing, anyway—and he never treated me differently because I was younger.

"I thought the world of him. He always inspired me to be my best self. We worked well together for two—almost three—years.

"On this particular assignment, we had thwarted a group that planned to throw an election in Spain. We should have been in the clear and heading for home. To this day, I'm not sure how we were found out. But we were, and we were captured.

"They took us to this building on the outskirts of Madrid. We were blindfolded. I never did have a clear idea of where we were, though it was an industrial area. When they took off the blindfolds, we were in some sort of nurse's office inside a factory complex. They brought us in and tied us to chairs. I did my best to keep the ropes loose, but whoever was tying me obviously knew what he was doing.

"The men who brought us there were not exactly pleasant, but their *jefe,* the boss, was furious at what we'd done. He came in and started yelling at us in Spanish—which I was sorry I understood at that particular moment. He hit Dix, hard, across the face, and made off-color remarks to him about me. Of course, we'd been trained not to respond, but it was difficult.

"Then he picked up two syringes and filled them with some nasty-looking yellowish liquid. He kept talking to

Dix, taunting him, the whole time, as if I wasn't really worth spending his time on. He said it was poison and it would kill us slowly. And painfully."

Agent Coltrane had closed her eyes. Her breathing was getting ragged with the memory. "There was yelling from outside the room, and the boss and the two thugs went running out. From the sound of it, they had dozens of people out there, many with guns—it would have been foolish to try to make a run for it. Dix had been able to pull his wrists free, and when they left, he was able to slip out of the ropes. He went to the cabinet; all he could find was benzodiazepine solution, but he figured it had to be better than what we had. He emptied one syringe into the sink and quickly refilled it with the solution. He had just returned that one to the tray and picked up the next one when we heard them coming back. He had to return the syringe with the poison still in it to the tray. In fact, it was all he could do to sit down and make it look like he was still tied up before they returned to the room. He was still struggling to get his hands in the ropes when he said to me, 'I'm sorry, Amber, I really am. You're going to have to get out of this by yourself. The benzodiazepine will just knock you out for a while, but the syringe is still contaminated with a trace amount of poison and you're probably going to wake up with some nasty headache.'

"I couldn't believe it . . . he was apologizing to me for using a contaminated syringe while he'd just consigned himself to death. I whispered, 'No!' It still seemed there had to be *something* we could do to make it out of there with both of us alive.

"The horrible boss man came back in, still very angry, and picked up the syringe that still had the poison in it. Dix said something purposefully provocative to him, so that the boss came over to Dix real fast and just jabbed the needle into him.

"I started to cry. The man was obviously done with both of us. He hardly even looked at the second syringe, certainly didn't notice the liquid was a slightly different color. As he was coming over to me, Dix said, 'Amber, look at me.' He held my gaze the whole time the *jefe* shoved the needle into my arm. 'You can do this,' he said. 'I love you, Am. And we succeeded.'"

I could hardly bear to look at Agent Coltrane. Tears were running down her face. "He was right, of course," she said. "Success and survival are two separate goals. We had stopped them from rigging the election. We had succeeded."

Agent Coltrane took a moment and centered herself.

"The *jefe* then growled, 'Dump them,' like we were garbage. He stalked out of the room. The two guards undid our ropes and forced us up at gunpoint. I was starting to feel dizzy, and I grabbed Dix for support as they forced us outside. There was like a hatch or cellar in the ground with a wooden door. They opened it, pushed us in, and padlocked it from outside.

"Dix did try to stand up and push against the door, but it was locked tight, and we were both running out of energy. We found each other in the dark and lay down together. Dix was stroking my hair to calm me, and I started to cry. I said thank you, but what can you say to someone who gave his own life to save yours?

"He told me not to cry, we all will die sometime, and this was a good way for him to go, a way he'd choose if he could. He said all he asked of me was to have a good life, to be happy when I thought of him, not sad.

"I told him I would always think of him with joy. I told him I loved him so much. And the truth was, I did. I'd been in love with him since the first day we'd met, but I'd always known it was never meant to be. But lying there in the dark, I kissed him, and he kissed me back. In fact, we chose to use the short time we had left to make love. Afterward, I could tell he was in pain, but he was so brave.

"I passed out before Dix did. I never saw him again."

I couldn't speak. I was so overwhelmed, I had nothing to say. Agent Coltrane looked so vulnerable and so sad. Even then, there was a small part of me that reveled in the fact that it was a relative of mine—my father— who had saved her life, who could create such intense emotion in her even now. Wait—my father . . .

A tremulous smile crossed her face. "Anyway. I woke up in a hospital bed, in a safe clinic back in the U.K. Dix had died by the time they found us. And as he predicted, I had the mother of all headaches. Like someone had dropped concrete bricks on my head.

"When I found out I was pregnant, I was honored to be carrying his child. It was the least I could do for him after he saved my life."

Her tone changed. She'd left the past, and was here, present, looking at me.

At this point, it became impossible for me to breathe.

"All the suits talked to me, Colt. They explained how much they needed me in the field. They talked about how Dix's parents were devastated by grief. How it would be joyful for them, and best for everyone, if they raised the baby. And my life is, well, pretty crazy. Eventually, I came to think maybe it was the right decision."

Now it was almost like she was afraid to look at me. Amber Coltrane. Afraid to look at me.

"I did stay with you for the first three months. It was such a wonderful time. And, of course, Lucy and Victor sent me pictures and e-mails all the time. And . . . I don't know if you remember, but when you were six or so, I played with you in a park when you were visiting California. I gave you a little stuffed otter."

The crazy thing was, in the recesses of my mind, I did remember. The nice lady in the park. It had been her. My mother. I probably still had that stupid otter, buried somewhere in the back of my closet. So I wasn't completely off when I felt like I had some connection to her.

She was quiet. I think it was freaking her out that I wasn't saying anything. But what on earth could I say?

"I know all of this must be overwhelming. I hope you'll forgive me for anything I could have done better. They have a counselor available to talk to you, whenever you'd like."

It was then that anger rolled through me—anger like I'd never known.

"So, it seems everyone else feels they have the authority to decide what my life should be. Who should be my parents. Where I should live. What lies they'd tell me." I heard myself screaming. I was shaking and trying not to cry. I felt so out of control, so betrayed. I certainly never went around yelling at grown-ups. Let alone my mother.

Amber Coltrane. My mother.

Somehow, she didn't get mad back. "I am so sorry about that part. I truly am."

"You're sorry? I have a mother, not just grandparents, but a mother, and you saw me once, in a park, in California? That's *all*?"

She was quiet. She looked at me and said, "It was so hard. Every day, it was so hard. But I believed what I was doing was best for you. Truly I did. That the best gift to give you was stability and a normal upbringing. And to go here, to Why? High, like I did. Like Dix did. Your dad. For you to grow up with a sense of belonging, not a terrible sense of loss."

"There are pictures of him everywhere! They said he was my brother. My hero brother. I grew up knowing I was nobody, nothing next to him. I could never compete. I'm hopelessly . . . I don't know what. Unremarkable. Not worth noticing. *That's* what you gave me! When . . . when . . . I was secretly special. At least my parents were! But nobody told me!"

I kept trying to calm down. I was fighting for breath. The mix of emotions was overwhelming.

"You didn't want me," I finally said, and when she started to protest, I cut her off. "You didn't want me *enough.*"

Agent Coltrane sat, looking at me. Not knowing what to say.

"I understand how it could feel that way. But I always wanted you. You have been a part of me, every single day. I was sixteen. I had no idea how to raise a child, especially since I was gone so much. No stability at all! And, you know what? I was friends with Dix, but I was also in awe of him. He was so courageous, and kind, and smart, and, well, wonderful. He was wonderful. I didn't know how to do that. How to raise a child to be like that. But his parents obviously did. And they were willing to do it again. They desperately wanted to do it again. All the love they had for Dix morphed into an even higher love for you.

"It wasn't the perfect solution. Maybe it wasn't even the best one. But I knew it wouldn't be forever. I knew this day, today, would come. And I was afraid of it . . . yet I was counting the seconds. When you'd have that firm foundation we all wanted to give you . . . but then, you'd also have me."

Silence crowded the room between us.

Finally, she continued. "I am just praying that you

can forgive me. That you will forgive me. You're angry now. And that's . . . all right. Whatever you're feeling, whatever you need to work through, is all right. I will help however I can. Or I will stay away. It's up to you. But, somehow, some way, when you're ready, I want to be in your life. However you'll let me in."

We stared at each other, sensing that we stood together at the start of a very long path.

Then I noticed a small smile, and she said, "You are in no way unremarkable. You're so like him. You're intuitive, and smart. Whatever crazy charisma Dix had, you have it too. I saw that from the get-go."

I was at a loss. Truly at a loss. I knew I would be sorting through all these roiling emotions for a very long time. Much of it was anger. But part of it was pride.

And part of me even thought this was very, very cool.

She looked away, and I wondered if all my anger had scared her off.

I was suddenly afraid she would go away again, and I would once again be motherless. Only now I would know that I was. Even though I was furious, I didn't want to lose her. I didn't want to irrevocably push her away.

"So," I finally said. "What do we do now?"

She looked back, and a small smile played hopefully

across her face. "Well," she answered, "I was hoping you might be free for lunch."

I said okay.

Domino three.

And that was how everything began.

CHAPTER FOUR

Cashew Chicken

WE DECIDED TO go casual and get some cashew chicken at the Hong Kong Inn on Battlefield Road. Truth is, I was hoping some of my friends from school might spot us there. Hours earlier, I had been merely one of the many who had been in awe of Agent Coltrane. Now we were out together sharing cashew chicken for two, which also came with fried rice, crab Rangoon, and fortune cookies.

Somehow, the fact that I had honestly expressed an impressive depth of anger, and she'd acknowledged it, let us put a bookmark in the huge emotional crater that had just blown open. We knew we'd be going back there, separately and together, for quite a while.

But as we left the school, we also entered into a tacit agreement that we'd give it a rest for the length of dinner.

I felt almost shy as we walked out to her car. Amber was driving a black convertible, with only two interior seats, both of which were red. It was low to the ground, aerodynamic, and looked like it should be called a Spyder or something, but it had a Swedish name, Koenigsegg, on the glove box. I'd never heard of it. She rolled her eyes and said it was all the rental car company had left at the airport. Amber Coltrane seemed like the kind of person for whom rental car companies would only have Spyders and cool Swedish convertibles left.

She was fun, and interesting, and interested in me. At the restaurant, we had a race to see who could finish his or her portion of rice first, using only chopsticks. She won by a mile, but I was assuming she had the unfair advantage of honing her skills in China. I acquitted myself pretty well.

When we were done, she casually said, "I'm going to use the restroom. Wanna pull up the car?"

I thought with lust about that black Spyder-thingy and said, "I'm only fifteen."

"I'll drive it on the street," she said. "Why don't you pull it around?"

Alrighty, then.

Domino four.

She threw me the key. I tried to act nonchalant as I sauntered back through the parking lot to the vehicle, using the key fob to unlock it. I climbed in and sat in the red bucket seat. It was gorgeous. Even the dash was soft leather.

Fortunately, I knew how to drive a stick. At school, we raced go-carts a lot, very cool go-carts. It was supposed to help with our coordination and reflexes. Like precision dance, only more fun. If I could keep the convertible dent-free for forty feet, I'd have done my job.

I pulled around front, staying well out of the way of the drive-through.

Agent Coltrane—which was how I still thought of her, I couldn't help it—came out and smiled when she saw me. Then, briefly, a thought flickered behind her eyes. She opened the door on the passenger side and got in.

"Colt," she said, calmly, "we don't have time to trade places. You need to do what I tell you, exactly what I tell you, when I tell you, and we'll be fine. Right now, drive to the exit to the street, but don't put on a turn indicator."

What?

"Now. Please."

I did as she asked. As I sat with the car idling by the busy street, I felt my adrenaline pumping. What was going on?

In a soft, firm voice she said, "Turn left."

You'd know it. Battlefield was five lanes here. Five busy lanes. But there was steel in her voice. I swung out to the left, into the center turn lane.

"Edge over one."

I did.

She was watching in the rearview mirror. She said, "Keep up with traffic. Go down to the next big intersection."

"In this lane?"

"I'll tell you when to change anything."

Oh, man, oh, man. Don't dent the car.

The straight-ahead light was green as we approached Campbell. There were four or five cars already waiting in the left-hand turn lane, which gave me the idea that our straight-ahead light was about to change. In fact, the green went out and the yellow lit up as I got there.

"Go through?"

"Yes," she said. And then, when I was in the middle of the intersection, "Make a U-turn. *Now.*"

Dear God. This was fourteen kinds of illegal. If a cop stopped me, I would never get my license. Ever.

The car didn't make a sound as I turned the wheel hard and drove in front of all those cars legally waiting for a left turn. Since the light was changing, there was no oncoming traffic.

So far, no cops.

"Stay straight. And drive."

I stayed straight. And drove. We hit red at the next corner. After that, we sailed through all the lights. After we passed the mall and entered a more residential neighborhood, she had me make a left on Luster and a right on Barataria, both of which were two lanes. Shortly thereafter, she swore softly under her breath.

"What's wrong?" I asked. "Company?"

"Seems that way," she said. "Make a right when you get to Lone Pine."

She reached across and hit the lever that automatically put the roof back on the convertible. Then she hit a circular silver button on the steering wheel.

"We're going to need a diversion," she said into it.

There was a pause of no more than five seconds before a male voice responded, "Two back?"

"Yes. Silver Mercedes."

"Come on in. We'll be waiting."

It seemed likely this wasn't a rental car.

I had never so much as taken a Volkswagen around the block. Now here I was, zipping along the curves of Lone Pine and making a left back onto Battlefield. The car did what I asked, and, surprisingly, was easier to handle than the go-carts. I was staying in the flow of traffic, not really passing anyone, and Amber wasn't asking me to. I thought I saw our tail, the Mercedes in question. It was staying one or two cars behind.

We continued on the main road. We passed under Route 65, which meant we were headed out of town, and in the direction of the school. Shortly thereafter, Amber had me make a left onto Farm Road 185, which was a nearly deserted two-lane road.

The Mercedes turned after us.

"We've called his bluff," Amber said. "Let's see what happens."

For a couple of miles, he stayed behind us. The road was straight, and there was no one else in sight in either direction.

Finally she said, "Okay, let's see how fast his model Mercedes can go. Take it to 130."

One hundred and thirty miles per hour? I looked at the speedometer. It was there, all right. I hit the gas. The car didn't exactly have to warm up. Within five seconds we were flying; in less than thirty seconds I'd reached 130. The Mercedes was screaming behind us.

"Don't go any faster," she said. "Let him catch us if he can."

It was a good thing, because the wind pressure was making it hard to stay straight. The car was vibrating, and it was all I could do to keep it pointed ahead.

The Mercedes accelerated also. I could see him out of the corner of my eye.

"Take it up to 140."

We began to pull away, but I was petrified. It felt like we were driving into a typhoon. I had the feeling that if I let go of the steering wheel, the car would shoot off into space.

The guy behind us tried to catch up. He almost did. But he couldn't, quite.

"Slow down. We need to turn right onto East Sunset."

I slowed down. I made it down to 65 miles per hour by the intersection. The car hugged the turn. Sixty-five I could handle. It was crazy exhilarating.

This was a busier street. I was still shaking a little bit, but was happy to stay at 65.

The driver of the Mercedes had had enough of biding his time. He sped up. I glanced back. There was someone in his passenger seat. Since I was in the left lane, the faster lane, the Mercedes passenger had to nearly climb out of the window to level his automatic weapon over the roof of the car. A rattle of bullets sliced the air over our car.

"Shit!" I said. My mother didn't correct me.

Just then, someone in a Mazda started honking like mad at the Mercedes and pulled in between us. It gave us another minute to pull away. We passed another intersection. Amber said, "Up here, as you probably know, Sunset turns back into a two-lane road. It suddenly starts winding into a forest. As soon as we hit the forest, speed up. But as soon as you reach the curve in the road, slow down immediately. Right after the turn, you'll be making a very hard left onto a dirt road. Got it?"

I nodded yes. The Mercedes had just about caught us when the big road ran out. I took the car up to 110. It was all I had time for before the curve. But it didn't matter. The driver of the Mercedes lost a good five seconds letting his passenger slide back down through the window into his seat.

I slowed down to 75 or 80. "There!" commanded Agent Coltrane.

I banked the steering wheel to the left and waited, breathless, praying for the car to make the turn without rolling. Once we were headed in the right direction, Amber said, "Floor it!"

I floored it. Only then did I look again at the speedometer. It went up to 245. We were flying, although nowhere near capacity speed. The car, as aerodynamic as it was, was shuddering as it pushed through the air in front of us. I didn't know whether to laugh or cry. I didn't even look at the speedometer, I just kept my eyes on the road and my hands glued to the steering wheel. One wrong bump, one squirrel in front of us, and we'd be history. We were nearly to the curve in the road. I had to slow down. I couldn't take it at this speed.

The car decelerated nearly as fast as it sped it. When we reached the forest and the road turned, I was down to a manageable 95.

"They're well behind us . . . that's perfect."

We turned another corner, and she said, "Slow down now."

We had to be getting near the school. We were driving along a concrete and rock wall that was about ten feet tall. There was another car farther up the road in front of us—a car exactly like ours. I saw a teenage boy and a woman in the bucket seats.

"Turn right, Colt!" Amber said. "Now!"

"What? The wall—"

"Drive into it. Here."

What? I turned the wheel as she'd demanded, heading straight at the wall at 90 miles an hour. At least the end would come fast.

It was all I could do not to take my hands off the steering wheel to shield my face.

The wall towered above us, and I drove smack into it.

CHAPTER FIVE

New Friends

AND THEN, THE wall was gone. I was on a segment of the go-cart track.

"Okay. You can stop now," Agent Coltrane said.

I knew this track. Like I was winding down a go-cart, I brought the Koenigsegg CCXR to a stop. As I did, I looked back. Where that segment of the wall had been, I could see straight through to the street. Outside, the Mercedes flew by, faster than ever. As I watched, the ground opened, and an exact match of the wall rose up.

"It's a hologram from the street side," Amber explained.

I had no idea the school compound had holograms.

"What was that other car on the road ahead?"

"It was a decoy of us. It was unfortunate we had to lead the bad guys back here. The other agents will lead them away and capture them, so we can at least know what's going on."

"Did you recognize the guys in the Mercedes?"

"I think so." She smiled at me. "Nice job driving. Great job, in fact."

"Thanks."

"Go ahead and drive on up and turn to the left." I did as she asked. We exited the go-cart track onto another road and disappeared into the trees. Eventually, the trees thinned and a clearing emerged. We came to the runway for the school's private planes. A small white jet with a blue stripe and a blue swirl on the tail was on the tarmac, its engines running.

"Is that for you?" I said.

"Yes."

The deflation I felt was enormous. So, that was it? After so many years, that was it? She flew in, had Chinese food, got chased by maniacs, then flew back out of my life?

"They want to get me out of here, just in case . . . I don't know. Just in case," she said.

In case those idiots in the Mercedes had friends who now knew her location.

She looked at the text on her cell. Then she looked back at me. "If you'd like, you can come with me. For a few days."

"Really?" I said. "I'd have to ask . . ."

"Victor and Lucy know. It's okay."

The stairs were down on the plane.

I shrugged. "Okay."

Domino five.

She gave me the "come on, then" sign and climbed up into the plane. I followed around to the other side, where the door was open. There were no propellers on this plane. It was tiny, like a personal jet. There was a pilot in the cockpit, but as we entered, he slid out of his seat and she slid into it. She pointed to the seat next to her. "That's you."

Holy cow.

"What kind of plane is this?" I asked.

"It's a Maverick. A SmartJet. Small but nice—and fast."

She shook the hands of the first pilot, who deplaned. She pressed a button and both doors began to close automatically. Agent Coltrane took the headset and put it on. She started talking to whoever ran

FALCON ground control. The engines revved and she pushed the lever forward. The plane headed for the runway.

I sat back as she started the taxi and easily lifted the plane up, into the sky.

It occurred to me that the teenager in the other car was probably Jonny Kryder. Pretending to be me. Because I had been in a high-speed chase with Amber Coltrane. A smile crept across my face.

I looked at the empty field below us. The city of Springfield grew smaller as we climbed. I sat back in my seat and tried to exhale.

So this is what it was like to have a mom.

In under an hour, we landed outside Chicago. This time the runway was wide and intersected with others.

"Is this airport all FALCON?" I asked.

"Yup," she said. "World headquarters."

I didn't see anything that looked remotely like a world headquarters. But back in Springfield, I hadn't seen anything that looked like a school, either.

Even now, I couldn't tell you exactly where the building was. We took a subway to get there. It wasn't a skyscraper; all the buildings in the compound were either one or two stories high. And it wasn't a square box, either. Inside the hallways bent as if they were circular.

Agent Coltrane and I walked long, light halls until we reached a glass-paneled wall, which slid open. Only it wasn't a wall. We'd walked onto an elevator car. Inside, there were plants but no buttons to press.

It went up. When we got off, we were met by a young man holding a tray on which were two sweating glasses of iced tea. Agent Coltrane took one. "Thanks, Ben," she said.

She turned and began walking across the carpeted floor toward a wall, which swung open as she reached it. I also took a glass of tea and followed her inside.

The office before us was welcoming. The far wall was windows, floor to ceiling, bowed slightly, which added to the evidence that the building was circular. Beyond the windows, perhaps ten miles away, the skyline of downtown Chicago glistened in the sun.

Before the windows was a cool desk made of a light-colored ash. Across the room were two sofas and several comfortable-looking chairs. Beyond them was what looked to be a wet bar, fridge behind it, ash-colored stools with black cushioned tops.

The gentleman who had been seated behind the desk

got up when he saw us and came around front. "Hello, Amber," he said.

"Hello, sir," she said. She turned to me. "Colton, this is Mr. Waverly. Mr. Waverly, Colt Shore."

I held out my hand, and he shook it, firmly.

"Come, sit down," he said. "I'm so pleased to meet you."

I took a gulp. Back at school, it was a hobby of ours to watch episodes of this 1960s television show called *The Man from U.N.C.L.E.* We loved it because it was so tongue-in-cheek, and because the agents' boss was named Mr. Waverly. We all thought it was funny because the real head of FALCON had the same name, though none of us ever expected to meet him.

Now here he was. Of course, he looked nothing like the dapper, aging Englishman played by Leo G. Carroll. Our Mr. Waverly was half Indian, in his fifties, and in very good physical shape. His first name was Ranjan.

"So, I hear you are a heck of a driver," he said, as Agent Coltrane and I sat down in the red chairs. He sat on the sofa.

"I . . . did my best," I said.

"It's a great thing to be cool under pressure," he said. "That can be taught to some extent, but it's so much easier if it comes naturally."

"Yes, sir, of course," I said.

"The driver of the other car was the person you suspected," he said to Amber. "We were able to bring both of them in. It seems you've gotten close enough to Phelan that we're starting to smoke them out."

"Great," she said.

"Glad you're here safely. We're using your intel—and this new information—to start to close in." Mr. Waverly turned again to me. "Colt, I'm really very pleased to meet you."

He stood up as he said this, and extended his hand again. I shook it, again. "Thank you. Very nice to meet you, also."

"I'm assuming you two have a few things to catch up on," he said to my mother. "We'll talk soon."

Amber shook his hand and we both left.

She texted the words "coming down" when we were in the elevator.

"Who's Phelan?" I asked.

"Very bad man. Involved in human trafficking."

"Oh." *And his henchmen had been chasing me through Springfield, Missouri?*

"Let's go to the workout room," she said.

Downstairs, as we passed a pleasant-looking café, she grabbed each of us a canteen with cold water and an energy bar. She used three more sets of pass codes and finally came to a staircase that descended past a tall wall of windows. She opened the door downstairs, and music floated out. I'm not sure if it was a joke meant to welcome me, but the song playing was "Secret Agent Man."

She entered the room to a cheerful chorus of "Amber!"

"Gentlemen, there's someone I'd like you to meet," she said, and she stepped sideways to reveal me behind her. "This is Colt."

No other introduction was apparently needed. There were three men in the room, and they quickly gathered around.

"Hello, Colt," said a blond man, perhaps six feet tall and wearing a large grin, which made his ripped muscles seem much safer. "It's great to meet you, kid."

"At long last," said the second, another well-built man, this one with jet-black hair and the English accent that had been missing from Mr. Waverly earlier.

"Hey, great to have you here," said the third, the youngest by far, in his mid-thirties, I judged.

"Colt, may I present Leif, Colin, and Tristan," she said.

There had been absolutely no need. There were certain agents in FALCON who were so legendary that all of us had heard of them and knew exactly who they were. These three gentlemen were easily at the top of the list. It was like, in U.N.C.L.E. lingo, walking into a gym to find Illya, Napoleon, and Mark Slate.

I worked hard on keeping my cool.

"We're big fans of your mom," said Colin.

"And we were great friends of your dad," said Leif.

"What are you thinking, Am?" asked Tristan, the youngest. "Are you in the mood to work out for a while, or shall we go get coffee and terrify the young man?" He winked at me to let me know he was kidding.

"We practically raised this one, then," said Colin, the dark-haired one, motioning to my mother.

"Which explains a lot," she muttered to me under her breath and grinned. Then she turned to the men and said, "Let me run for half an hour, then let's get out of here," she said.

I decided I might as well work out too. Each of us at the school had a personal trainer who had plotted an individual workout course for us. Amber pointed to the men's dressing room and I found shorts and a white T.

We all worked out for half an hour. It was a riot. The music was definitely secret-agent-based, although from the amount of laughter it solicited, I guessed it wasn't their normal soundtrack.

After half an hour, Mom called it quits and grabbed a towel from her elliptical machine. "Race you to be dressed and ready," she said. As the others grabbed towels also, someone's phone—or text message, or whatever—went off. It was a distinctive ring. Later I found out they all recognized it as an urgent summons to Waverly's office.

It was almost comical, watching the four of them locate their devices and one by one determine the call wasn't for him. But when Mom picked hers up, it was clear it had been her device that had gone off. She blew hair out of her face as she turned it on.

And, for the first time since I'd met her, Agent Coltrane momentarily lost her cool. She looked up toward the three men who stood around her, waiting for the news.

"It's him," she said. "He wants Colt."

CHAPTER SIX

The Fast Track

WHEN AMBER AND I got off the elevator on Mr. Waverly's private floor, Ben smiled and said, "He's waiting for you."

This was addressed to me.

I looked at Agent Coltrane, who nodded and said, "I'll wait here."

The door slid open, and I walked once more into the lion's den.

All of this would have been completely unnerving if I'd been waiting for months to fly to Chicago for an appointment to meet Mr. Waverly. Now, however, it seemed like the next act in an incredibly surreal play that required audience participation. The door slid shut behind me with a soft *swoosh,* and I waited to see what would happen next.

"Hello again, Colt," Mr. Waverly said, standing and moving toward me from behind his desk. This time, he claimed a chair, and I sat catty-corner to him on the sofa. He was lean and well muscled. Apparently, working out was a popular pastime around here.

"Sorry, I was in the middle of something last time you were here, so we didn't get to spend much time together. Coincidentally, there might be something with which you may be able to help."

Mr. Waverly picked up a thin, rectangular device called a holopad that was about the size of an iPad. He glanced at it.

"It says here you're an expert on the countries bordering the Mediterranean."

"Yes, sir." That simple statement was loaded. It said I wasn't on an "active" track; I was headed for the think-tank side of things. And, as important as the planners and creative thinkers would be to making the world a better place, it was definitely sidekick status.

"And you're a third-degree black belt in Tae Kwon Do."

"Yes, sir." Seeing as how we all started martial arts in kindergarten, third-degree was pretty much standard by my age.

He scrutinized the screen further. "We miss your dad," he said. "And we highly value your mother."

"Yes, sir."

He put the device down and looked at me. "Have you ever considered going active?"

There it was. The question that each of us fantasized coming from our track counselor, so overwhelmed with our potential that we'd be asked to kick it up a notch. An interesting hypothetical question.

Now, of course, the hypothetical part was out the door. My first reaction was, of course I'd considered it. Everyone had. My second: He thinks he's talking to my hero dad. I'm not him. Not even close. Do I tell him now? Do I let this go any farther?

"Yes, sir."

"The situation at hand has nothing to do with countries bordering the Mediterranean. It has to do solely with the fact that we need someone with a cool head, who's well trained in defensive arts, who can blend into the situation."

"Blend in?"

He'd pulled up a snapshot on his device. It was a

group of boys hanging out. They looked to be about my age. One of them looked familiar, but any of them could have been among my group of friends. A drum kit was in the background, and one of the boys held an electric guitar.

"You remind me of this young man," Mr. Waverly said. I looked more closely. The boy looked to be about my age, but his face was rounder, his eyes smaller. It was the hair that did it. We had the same cut.

"There is a kidnap threat against one of the other young men in this photo. He travels widely, and is about to make another trip. There will be a professional bodyguard with him and his sister at all times, but we need someone on the inside, just in case."

Mr. Waverly looked over at me. "Let me make this clear: you do not have to do this. We can use someone else. You should in no way feel pressured. But you do have the training necessary, and you look younger than any of the available active agents. Also, please don't feel pressured by the fact that I'm the one asking you. It could be that you're called to do something else altogether and this would sideline that calling. Or it could be you're meant to go active, just not now. Only you know the answer to that."

There was a moment's silence.

"What are you thinking?"

The real answer was I was thinking *I'm not Dix, I'm the also-ran.* But, surprisingly, this was superseded by thoughts of Malin James, that girl in our school who, as you may recall, was pretty and built, laughed a lot, and was genuinely nice. Why had she been looking at me in the café?

She was completely out of my league. If there were such a thing as leagues at Why? High, Jonny Kryder was captain of one, and I was smack in the middle of the other. Not that Malin had fallen for Jonny; she was too real for that. Nor had she ever been dismissive of me. Really, except that one time, she had never noticed me, one way or the other. Basically because I'd done nothing to either merit or arrest her attention. In the cool or noteworthy department, I held no currency. I was biding my time.

Being sent on a case by Mr. Waverly could bring my time closer in a hurry.

On the other hand, supposing I went to secretly guard this guy and something actually happened? Was I ready to have that kind of responsibility? Someone's life could be at stake.

But did I not just drive a car through a wall? Was I not the son of Amber Coltrane and Dixon Shore? That alone kicked my answer up to *Hell, yes.*

Right?

"I'm thinking it would be an honor," I said.

Mr. Waverly smiled.

Domino six.

He hit a button at the back of his desk, and suddenly another man in a suit was standing near me in the middle of the room. I saw the projection lights on the floor. From his hologram he looked very businesslike. Ginger-brown hair, tie slightly undone.

"This is Mr. Davis," Mr. Waverly said. "Charles, let me introduce you to Colt Shore. He has agreed to assist the Ellis family."

"Very good," said Mr. Davis. He also held a holopad with the same photo Mr. Waverly had just shown me. A hologram of a holopad. Interesting.

He turned the screen with the photo back to me. "This young man," he pointed to a tall boy next to the one with my haircut, "is a musician named Thorne Ellis. He and his sister, Talya, are musicians."

The minute he said Thorne's name, I realized why I'd recognized him. Thorne and Talya were talented musicians who had a well-known band called Shadow. Although they were still teenagers, they'd managed to avoid the Disney/Nickelodeon pop music jungle and were known for doing edgy, jazz-infused rock, most of which they wrote themselves or with their band. While Talya looked like she could choose to be a pop princess, I'd been surprised last summer to see her participating in an extreme-sports program for charity. She'd been skateboarding, doing half-pipes and fifty-fifty grinds with the best of them. I think she also dove off a hundred-foot cliff. Strange girl. Wicked talented, though.

"Their parents are both journalists. Their dad, Stuart, covers mostly Southeast Asia. Their mom, Sophie, is currently in Afghanistan. Thorne and Talya's band has been scheduled to do a USO tour there. However, apparently their mother has been doing more than the puff pieces the Taliban and the insurgents want her to do. They've threatened to kidnap her children if she doesn't stop writing the truth about what she's been finding out."

"Why don't they postpone their tour?" I asked.

"Good question," said Mr. Waverly. "The truth is, the threat was made against them that they would be kidnapped no matter where in the world they are. In

Afghanistan, they'll be very well protected. And they fully support their mother's work. They don't want to make it look like they've been intimidated."

"So, what would I do?"

Mr. Davis said, "You'd blend in as one of Thorne's friends and travel with them to Afghanistan. We'd brief you on the culture and on the group that's threatening Sophie Ellis and what to look out for."

Mr. Waverly asked, "What do you think? Are you up for it?"

Go hang out with one of my favorite rock groups and go with them into Afghanistan? "I'm up for it," I said.

Domino seven.

"Thank you, Charles," Mr. Waverly said, and *zoop!* the hologram of Charles was gone.

Mr. Waverly smiled and stood up. "As you know, technically, everyone who attends the academy has been given permission by their parents and/or legal guardians to do anything asked of them by FALCON. However, in this particular instance, I believe both you and I had better clear it with your mother before making a final decision. And you do have until tomorrow morning to change your mind.

"That said, Thorne and Talya's group, Shadow, is due to leave for Afghanistan in three days, so we've got to get someone over there in the morning. We'll start prepping you immediately, unless you change your mind."

I stood up also. "Thank you, sir. I won't change my mind."

He shook my hand. "I'm assuming that's true, and we'll get you going," he said, but then he cocked his head toward the hallway. "However, you've only just now met your mother. She can be a very determined woman. Give me first crack at her," he said with a slight smile. "We'll see how this all shakes down."

CHAPTER SEVEN

Tethers

WHAT I THOUGHT was, *There's no problem. My mother is Amber Coltrane, one of his top agents. She'll be proud of her son being sent on his first mission at fifteen.*

What I should have thought was, *Good heavens, even Mr. Waverly seems slightly intimidated by my mother.*

She was waiting when I came out of the office. Instead of talking to me, she strode straight toward Mr. Waverly. He must have been expecting this, because I didn't hear any expressions of surprise before the door swooshed closed behind her.

I didn't have time to dwell on this, as a tall gentleman

in his fifties was waiting for me in the outer office. He wore a gray suit, blue shirt. "Grayson," he said, offering his hand, which I shook. "I'm your tether. Come along."

Ben gave a farewell nod as I headed for the elevator with Mr. Grayson.

An agent's tether is his or her liaison between FALCON and the current assignment. This is the person who gets you pertinent information, monitors your movements and the situation, and makes sure you have what you need to get the job done and get safely home.

"So, if you're my tether, who's my partner?" I asked.

"This isn't a proactive assignment," he said. "You don't have a partner; you'll have backup."

"Oh," I said. Apparently there were a few things I'd missed by not taking Fieldwork 101.

"It's three o'clock now. Your first briefing is at three forty-five."

"All right."

We were going through long, curving hallways. Mr. Grayson walked at such a fast clip it was all I could do to keep up with him without trotting. We came to a wider bank of elevators, went down two levels, and then continued our walk.

He finally slowed outside a suite of rooms with a sign on the door that said "Health Initiatives." He tapped a button beside the door and we entered.

A fit woman, slightly shorter than I, with salt-and-pepper spiked hair, waited inside. Like most grown-ups in FALCON, she was so fit it was hard to guess at her age. Older than my mom, that was as close as I got. She also held a holopad.

"This is Colton?" she asked.

"It is indeed," answered Grayson.

"World-ready, first stop Afghanistan?" she asked.

"That's it," he said.

"Right this way," she said to me. "I'm Maggie Verhagen, your wellness coordinator."

"What does that mean, world-ready?" I asked, following her off into an interior hallway.

"Once an agent is active, she or he often starts in one country, but who knows where you'll actually end up? We'll prepare you to stay healthy, wherever you are. Unfortunately, you're leaving on assignment so soon that we're going to have to start with what I call best-guess technology." She smiled. "I've looked at your records. You've got a good start."

FALCON certainly had cutting-edge medical technology, blending Western medicine, chiropractic, and holistic practices. Which still didn't make the next twenty minutes' worth of vaccinations fun. I only briefly regretted the enthusiasm with which I'd agreed to go active. Dr. Verhagen carefully explained every medication I was receiving, and she also gave me a quick-fix kit at the end, again explaining what pills were for what situations. She also did a chiropractic alignment, which I hadn't realized I needed, but really helped. I'd also heard that active agents were allowed to have massages as often as would be helpful. Which, after high-speed car chases and rushing around in personal jets, could be needed fairly often. At least in my opinion.

When Dr. Verhagen cheerfully led me back to the central room, considerably worse for the wear, I was surprised to find Mr. Grayson was gone.

Instead, the only person in the room was Colin Restive, one of the three top agents Amber Coltrane and I had been working out with earlier. As soon as the doctor handed me off, he said, "Slight change of plans. You've got a new tether, and I'm him."

Colin Restive. My tether. It was mildly like hearing, "Hi, my name is James Bond. I'll be your server tonight." I wasn't even supposed to be "proactive" on this assignment. I could only imagine the conversation that must have transpired between my mother and Mr. Waverly.

As we walked together into the hall, my phone vibrated with a text message. We both paused, and he indicated it would be okay if I read it.

It was from my friend Luke. "Where R U??" it read. "U left class & disappeared!" I looked up at Colin. "It's from my friend in Springfield. I don't know . . . how much I can say."

"Good question," said Agent Restive. "Let's have a seat," he said. We'd come to a place where four hallways converged. It had some huge potted plants and circular chairs. He indicated the chairs, and we sat.

He took a deep breath and leaned forward, so that no one passing could hear us.

"Your mum has had very bad luck with loved ones who are active agents—specifically her dad and yours. It's hard for her to see her way clear to putting you in the line of fire."

"That's not fair, is it?" I asked. "My only surviving parent puts herself 'in the line of fire' every day, but she nixes it for me?"

"I didn't say it was fair," Colin said. "I wanted to

let you know where she was coming from. You'll make more headway if you can sympathize with her point of view."

"But I can go, can't I?"

Even in a polo shirt and jeans, which Agent Restive had changed into after our workout, he exuded both nonchalance and power, simultaneously. Meeting him at a newsstand or at the laundromat, you'd guess he had to be a diplomat or a movie star. And it wasn't just his muscles, his great head of jet-black hair, or his English accent, though none of those things went any way toward disguising his intrinsic coolness.

"Well, you've gone through the first round of vaccines, which is arguably the worst part. It would be fairly ruthless to stop you now." He gave a crooked smile. "No matter what, if you go active, you're not going to be able to tell anyone that Amber is your mom. The four of us you've talked to today—Mr. Waverly, Leif, Tristan, and myself—and, of course, your grandparents—know. But it can't go any farther than that, especially if you're being sent into the field. The minute word gets out, you both become targets. You would be a perfect kidnap target for someone wanting something from your mother, and vice versa. So it has to be kept quiet. Can you understand why?"

I did. But it was a bummer.

"Can people know that I've gone active, at all?"

"Certainly. It will be obvious when your courses change at school."

"And people can know . . . that I *know* Agent Coltrane?"

"They can see that you're best of friends."

At least that was something. I sat back. "So she doesn't want me to go?"

"Not at all."

"What should I do?"

"Be respectful of her feelings. But do what you must."

We sat looking opposite directions down the hall. I was grateful for whatever had happened that had switched my tethers. I had the feeling, as capable as he was, I wouldn't have been able to have this conversation with Mr. Grayson.

Agent Restive checked his watch.

"Shall we head for your briefing?" he asked.

I stood up. "Yes." Then, with greater sureness, "Yes."

Before we left, I handed him my phone, so he could see what I'd typed to Luke. "I've gone active. Out of touch, but will fill you in when I return," I'd typed.

"Fine," he said, and I pressed Send.

As we started off, he said, quietly, "If there's a friend

you trust with your life, you may tell him or her about your mother," he said. "Technically, you shouldn't. But it's important that you feel there are trusted friends who truly know you. You must choose wisely, and be very discreet. It must be as though no one knows."

"Yes, sir, I understand," I said as we continued to walk. "Thank you."

CHAPTER EIGHT

Briefing

THE BRIEFING ROOM was perhaps twelve by twelve. I thought we'd be sitting at a table, with maps all around, but there were no maps. Instead, we sat in comfortable swivel chairs, facing the woman and the man who'd been awaiting us.

They introduced themselves, and the woman said, "Let's begin."

She pressed a button on a remote, and the entire interior wall lit up as a screen. On it was a map of the world. She went up and pinched Afghanistan, and it grew larger as we zoomed in. "We've been supporting a journalist named Sophie Ellis, who's been investigating and reporting on women's issues in Afghanistan. Much of what she's reported has been positive—the opening of schools and so forth. Lately, there have been a number of orchestrated incidents, including gassing and poisoning of female students and teachers, and other intimidation techniques. These kinds of things we attribute to the Taliban and other conservative religious forces. The Taliban has been quite angry at Sophie, but she has been careful and has done her best not to cross too many lines. However, in her investigations, it seems she's come upon some other kinds of corruption. She's been able to send us vague reports, but she's been out in the middle of nowhere without any kind of secure communications."

As the woman said this, she tapped the holopad screen and a photo of a pleasant-looking American woman popped up on the wall. She had silvering hair, dark eyes, and an oval face, and she wore a headscarf. What caught my attention was the look in her eyes. She was intelligent and determined, someone you didn't mess with unless you knew what you were doing.

"This is Sophie Ellis. Her two children, Thorne and Talya, are musicians with a popular band called Shadow." A photo of the band came up on the screen next to Sophie.

"Are you familiar with their music at all?" Angela asked.

I nodded.

"Great. Anyway, they've been scheduled to do a USO tour in Afghanistan. It hasn't been announced or promoted. But somehow, someone knows they're coming and has told Sophie that if she continues her current line of investigation, her children will be in danger.

"But the kids are determined to go. I think, partly, they're worried about their mom and want to get over to her. So. Current assignment, blend in with Thorne's friends. You'll need to act as a roadie to explain why you've gone along. They will travel with their usual bodyguard, and there will be military protection. But keep your eyes and ears open. You may also be called on to facilitate getting some of Sophie's secret material back to us."

She turned and looked me in the eyes. "Sound doable?"

"Absolutely," I said, with more certainty than I felt, although it sounded like my part wasn't so hard, as long as others got me to the right place at the right time.

"Great. You'll head for New York, where the Ellis kids live, in the morning, then."

"They know I'm coming?"

"They will. Good luck. "

With that, she swept out the door.

Colin and I remained seated.

"So," I said, "what's next?"

"Don't you watch spy movies? What's always next?" Agent Restive asked. There was a twinkle in his eye. I had a feeling he didn't do this very often, and he was getting a kick out of it.

I thought of the quick jazz interlude that played in between scenes on *The Man from U.N.C.L.E.*

"A travel sequence?" I asked.

He laughed. "Not quite yet. I think you need some gadgets."

As he spoke, the door slid open and a different man and a woman walked in. She was pretty, for a grown-up, with dark eyes and dark hair pulled back into a barrette. He looked to be about the same age, was slightly balding, but looked happy and fairly pleased to be there. The woman carried a briefcase. She set it down on the table.

"Colton Shore?" she asked, though, really, who else would I be? Then she noticed that Agent Restive was there. She smiled at him, and the man said, "Why, Colin," and shook his hand. So everyone else was as impressed as I was that he was my tether.

"I'm Anna," said the woman, "And this is Paul. We've got a few things for you—"

I must have looked disappointed without meaning to, because she quickly added, "But they're great things. In fact, we'll spend the next half an hour or so trying to get you comfortable with as many of the applications as possible."

"The first is your phone." She handed it to me. It looked like a typical smart phone, same shape and weight. It didn't have a logo, so I couldn't tell if it was an Apple or Windows based, or something else altogether. "It looks a lot like my phone," I said, pulling mine out of my pocket for comparison.

"It is a lot like yours," said Paul. "We go on the assumption that phones are easily lost or stolen, the first things taken from you if you're ever captured, so it looks and acts very much like a normal phone. It takes high-resolution photos and videos, you can either speak or type your texts, it's a universal GPS, which means we can locate it anywhere, and it can direct you out of anywhere. It can understand what you're saying. The phone works in any country, and it plays music. Almost every application that we were proud of handing to our agents ten years ago is now for sale to anyone with an Internet-ready phone. These days, the difference is in what we can do with the information on our end, once you send it to us."

"For example." Anna picked up the phone and snapped my picture. She sent it somewhere, and within seconds received a message back. She showed it to me. It had my photo, and underneath it displayed my name, birth date, and other information.

"If you send us a photo of someone, we can use face-recognition software and get back to you, usually in under a minute, identifying the person. We also have voice-recognition software, where we can identify many voices, though the database isn't nearly as large."

"Although, now that you're active . . ."

Anna snapped a photo of Colin, and when the info came back, she showed it to me. "Subject unrecognized."

"All active agents are either unrecognized or given a mission-useful identity," she said. "You'll be moved to the active database once we leave you now."

"Cool," I said.

"And here," she said, this time handing me a ring. It had a gold band with a black onyx stone inset. "It's what they call tiger-eye," Anna continued, "which explains the design in the onyx."

I put it on my ring finger on my left hand. It fit fine.

Only then did I notice a small protrusion, like a button, on the bottom.

"Ah, you found it," said Paul. "If you press the ring against someone's skin and click twice, then hold the button down, the ring injects them with a drug that will cause unconsciousness almost immediately. It also leaves no puncture wound, so it's virtually untraceable."

I held my hand out in front of me and admired the ring. I had never worn one, but it looked good.

"You'll want to come up with a good story of where you got it and why you wear it," said Anna, "since boys your age don't usually wear rings. Also, here are a couple of disks that will serve as tracking devices if you can place them on a person or thing you need to follow."

Then she smiled. "Finally . . ."

Paul came forward with a box and put it on the table in front of me. I glanced at Colin. He was smiling too.

I opened the box. There was a watch with a silver band and a black face. It looked fashionable but hardly unusual. The one unexpected thing was that instead of one knob for adjusting the time, it had three knobs: one in the center, one at the top left, and one at the bottom left.

It looked distinctive, but wouldn't call undue attention to itself, which was what I guessed they were going for.

They were all still looking at me, grinning. I picked it up, hesitantly, like there must be something more to it than I knew.

"It's your watch," said Paul proudly.

"Okay . . ."

"It means you're an active agent," Colin explained. "A version of this—in fact, they each look different on purpose—is presented to every agent just before his or her first mission. You might swap out the ring or the phone from case to case, but the watch stays with you."

I took it out of the box and pressed one of the buttons. Nothing happened.

I looked up expectantly.

"Put it on," said Anna.

I did.

"Try it again."

This time, when I hit the same button, the watch's face lit up, and three different screens appeared. "Wow," I said.

"Do you remember when the doctor put the scratchy bandage on your arm?" Paul asked.

Did I? When she ripped it off, it really smarted. Like it took skin with it. "Yeah."

"That gave us the pH balance of your skin, blood type; actually, checked off fourteen different boxes. All that information was transferred to this watch. Because of that, it recognizes your skin, and only your skin. If you take it off, or if anyone else puts it on, it's a normal, battery-powered watch," said Paul.

"But on you . . ." Anna smiled again.

"There's practically nothing it won't do."

To prove the point, we spent the next fifteen minutes putting the watch through its paces. It did many of the same things the phone did: it was a GPS and a telephone that could call Colin (or headquarters) at any time and scramble the conversation. It had a panic button that I could press if I was ever in dire trouble—I asked if ninjas would jump out of the watch, but they hadn't perfected that application yet. It was a flashlight, a laser cutter, and a sonar with light-up arrows should I ever be trapped in a pitch-black cave.

"Once you're old enough to drive, it will also run a company car by voice command," said Paul.

I was tempted to mention that I was only here because I'd recently outrun bad guys in a high-speed car chase.

Anyway, the watch felt cool against my wrist. I mean, the steel literally felt cool.

"Thanks," I said.

With that, Paul and Anna each shook my hand and left.

I looked at the watch. I'd have to get used to it telling me the time instead of using my cell phone as a pocket watch like everyone else. Surprisingly, it was after five.

"What now?" I asked.

Colin looked at his watch—his agent watch, which I now recognized as having several extra buttons, as did mine. And he said, "I think we go to dinner with your mom."

CHAPTER NINE

With the Band

LESS THAN TWENTY-FOUR hours after I was sitting in class in Springfield, Missouri, I was in a FALCON jet on my way to New York City, accompanied by a specialist in Arab cultures. We spent the trip talking about Afghanistan. Given the fact that I was about to go there and attempt to not inadvertently offend any of the locals, the ride from Chicago to New York seemed incredibly short.

Once in Manhattan, I was handed off to the band's manager, Bengal Driver. Bengal was a thin young man with a small silver nose ring, shaggy hair, and an attitude that said, "I'm the creative muscle looking out for the young artistes."

As we got on an elevator in the lobby of their practice studio on West Twenty-eighth Street, he asked, "So, have you heard any of the band's music?"

We both stood facing the elevator door as we ascended. "Yes," I said. "They've got some great stuff. I've learned the drum parts on some of their songs."

And I immediately thought, *What an incredibly lame thing to say.* Sort of like a singer saying, "I do karaoke of their stuff at the bowling alley every Thursday." Why would any real musician care?

So when we reached the practice room, it was with horror that I heard Bengal announce, "Hello, kiddies. Meet Colt Shore. Your drummer for the USO gig."

The whole band was there. I recognized each of them. Thorne played bass guitar; his sister Talya played guitar. They had a second (world-class) guitarist, a killer keyboardist, and a famous drummer named Rip Ettinger.

I was frozen to the spot. Instead of being thrilled to meet Rip Ettinger, I was now mortified. He was a stylist and an innovator. I was fifteen. I knew it was a joke Bengal had just made, but it was a bad one.

"Okay, that's it, then," said Thorne, and they all put

down their instruments. "Darrell, Talya, take a break. Oscar, see you in a week."

Oscar, the other guitarist, packed up his stuff.

"This is Darrell Van Dyke," Bengal said of the keyboardist, who was heading out for a half-hour break. "And this is Talya," Bengal said.

Talya Ellis was an insanely talented musician and composer. Other artists had started recording her stuff when she was fourteen. She was now sixteen. Talya was striking on album covers, but nothing did justice to her effortless beauty in person. She wore no makeup, and her long black hair had natural curl. She was wearing jeans and a green tank top that did wonders at both covering and revealing what lay beneath.

She didn't even acknowledge me as she brushed by. In fact, she looked downright hostile.

It was Thorne who came over and shook my hand. Her brother was a year older and also had jet-black hair. Thankfully, he also had a friendly smile that resonated in his eyes.

"Hello, Colt," he said. "Thanks for joining us."

"You're welcome," I said. "Although it seems your sister isn't exactly happy to have me here."

Thorne, who was a good three inches taller than I was, pulled me over to the side of the room. "Don't pay any attention to her. She doesn't admit it, but she's got a thing for Rip, our drummer."

Cold dread rained through my insides. "Listen, what your manager said about me being the drummer—"

"It's a godsend that you can play the drums. If this was just a regular USO tour, fine, the whole band could go, and then some. But we're slated to go to some smaller FOBs—forward operating bases—not to mention we have another purpose as well. It's four band members, max. So if you didn't play an instrument, we would have had to jettison either drums or keyboards besides Oscar, with no replacement. As it is, our drummer's sister is getting married next week. He's more than fine with sitting this one out. And it's Talya who's insisting we go deeper into Afghanistan. We haven't been able to contact our mom for the last few days. Talya is determined to get there ourselves, locate her, and get her to come home with us."

Sophie Ellis was *missing*? Why had I not been told this? Was this new information? There was no time to confer with Colin. Thorne was pressing on.

He paused. "Okay, that last part was me. I want to get Mom the hell out of there. But we're both determined to find her. And since you can play the drums, that means we get to have both drums and keyboard for the concert. Yay. So don't pay any attention to my sister. She's grateful you're coming along. Or she will be."

Rip had gotten a giant can of one-half iced tea and one-half lemonade with a picture of Arnold Palmer on it and had come back to his Yamaha kit.

I made my way back, and he indicated that I should sit on his drum throne. He handed me a pair of his own drumsticks.

"What songs do you know?" Thorne asked.

They certainly didn't have time to teach me more than a couple more songs, so the ones I already knew would dictate their playlist.

I named a couple of their tunes I'd worked out, including, ironically, the one I'd been figuring out when I'd overheard my uncle and grandparents talking.

"Okay, let's see what you've got," Rip said.

I wasn't even warmed up. As I nervously centered myself, and as Thorne went to the keyboards to play along, it occurred to me that this was either a dream come true or my worst nightmare come to life. I hadn't decided which.

Thorne hit the opening chords, and I began to play.

Apparently, they decided I was good enough to fill in for a three-day, unrecorded tour in the middle of a war zone. Thorne, Rip, and I spent most of the day working on four other songs. I had a feeling Rip was simplifying some of the parts, but that was more than fine with me.

That night I went back with Thorne and Talya to their house in New Jersey. It was maybe forty minutes from the Holland Tunnel, in an upscale suburb. The house was nice but not flashy; apparently, it was where they had grown up. Since their dad was in Pakistan and their mom was in Afghanistan, it was just us and one bodyguard, which made me really nervous. I wasn't sure when the threat against them would kick in—or if it had already. The bodyguard stayed on the main floor, while Talya went upstairs to her room and Thorne and I went downstairs into their finished basement, which looked out onto a landscaped yard with a pool. We drank more Arnold Palmers and talked until late, about nothing, really—which other bands we liked, good movies we'd found by accident on cable, stuff like that. After midnight, we both went up to bed. I don't know if he slept.

I did not.

Which was probably why, after Thorne, Talya, Darrell, Bengal, Deek the bodyguard, and I boarded the Gulfstream G550 at Teterboro Airport and headed for Paris, I found a seat in the front of the aircraft and fell fast asleep. Until someone plopped across from me somewhere over the Atlantic Ocean and said "Hey, Spy Guy."

I don't know if I was more annoyed at being awakened or by how Talya had been treating me, but I answered, "I'm not a spy, I'm an agent. There's a difference. I'm protecting you, not that you seem to be grateful."

"You're protecting me. How old are you, anyway?"

"Fifteen."

"Fifteen? You can't even drive!"

"I can drive," I responded. "It's just that certain officers say I *may* not drive."

"WTF?" she said. "We're going into Afghanistan, and they've sent a pre-driver."

Pre-driver? Was that even a word? And I was here specifically because Talya and Thorne were so young. "I thought you were sixteen," I said.

"I can drive," she responded haughtily.

"So it's all about driving?" I replied testily. "Last time I heard, this particular job was about protecting you and Thorne against a kidnapping threat, and blending in so no one will suspect me. I've been training for stuff like this since I was five." Sort of. Just on the wrong track, but she didn't need to know that.

"I've been a musician since I was three."

"I guess you win, then." Back in Springfield, when I'd

dreamed about meeting Talya Ellis, our first conversation had gone nothing like this. I took a breath and tried a change of tone. "Except, well, it shows that you've been working that long. You're a very talented musician."

There was no response to the compliment. "So they said nothing to you about finding my mother?" she asked.

I didn't know what to say. When I'd told Colin she was missing, he sounded surprised. "It didn't come up."

She leaned forward and said, somewhere between a whisper and a hiss, "My mother is doing very important and very dangerous work, trying to help the women of the world, particularly those in Afghanistan. Do you even know anything about the situation, Spy Guy?"

"I know some," I said. "I know that the Taliban and other conservative clerics feel women should be kept completely subservient, and have been waging terror-battles against these things; they've recently been gassing the girls' schools and sending pupils and teachers to the emergency room. It's an uphill battle, and I completely support your mother's work bringing the situation to the world's attention."

"You can't appreciate the danger she may be in even now."

This was touching a nerve with her. Obviously, she was very worried about her mom.

"I think I can understand," I said. "My father was killed being a 'Spy Guy,' as you call it."

I wasn't allowed to talk about my own mother, but no one had said anything about keeping my father a secret.

This final statement caused her to sit back. She was quiet for a minute.

"Sorry," she mumbled. I could see her cogs of thought braiding and turning. "What did you mean when you said that being a spy and being an agent were different things?"

"Spies try to stop bad guys. Agents—at least, the kind I am—are more concerned with supporting the good guys. Like your mom."

"But aren't you trying to stop the bad guys from kidnapping us?"

"Yeah. In support of your mom. I'm trying to support the good guys by keeping their kids from being kidnapped."

"It seems like you've given this some thought."

"I have a class in it—philosophy, morality, situation ethics. Every year."

"And how about Islam? What do you know about Islam?"

I knew she was asking because various factions of

that religion were running the country where we were headed.

"Quite a lot, actually. At my school, we study all the major religions, and how they're practiced in different parts of the world."

There was a reason she was making me jump through these hoops, and I wished she'd just tell me what it was.

"So you study them all and believe none?"

"To the contrary. Once a FALCON agent has decided what he or she believes, he or she delves deeply into that religion to try to understand and live its precepts fully." I closed my eyes. This was so hard to explain to a civilian. "We're supposed to understand what we believe and live by it. The point is to make us each fully integrated human beings."

"While making you a third-degree black belt."

"Yeah," I said. "And I can also *drive*."

"So, what religion are you?"

"I'm a Christian. We're big on justice, love, peace, and humility. I'm especially good at the last one." I hoped she knew that was a joke.

"How many languages do you speak?"

"Only three."

"لرل امید (*umīd laral*)," she said.

I didn't understand, but I knew she was speaking

Pashto, the major language of Afghanistan. I'd studied rudimentary phrases for an hour on the flight to New York.

"Wazhay yam," I answered. *I'm hungry.*

"That's good. It's time to eat," she said.

She got up and moved back to the sofa and comfy chairs, where the others were being served a tasty-looking soup, sandwich, salad, and dessert. I realized I was starving.

"Colt, come on," said Thorne, waving me over.

I stood stiffly and stretched. I knew from her questions that Talya was planning something that wasn't currently on our itinerary, and she was trying to sort out who would be of help. Had she found me qualified? Did I want her to find me qualified?

"Take one step at a time," Colin had told me. I took a breath and decided to deal with what was currently in front of me, which, thankfully, was lunch.

o o o

Our first concert, in Kabul, was off the hook. Thorne and Talya knew how to work the crowd. Two thousand soldiers stomping, clapping, cheering for Shadow. And me, sitting on stage, playing drums.

Seriously.

We had gotten on a C-17 airplane at the Air Force base in Kuwait. It was like a hollowed-out, two-story flying tunnel. We were strapped in seats along the sides. If I could ask Jonny Kryder, the kid at my school who was also an active agent, one thing, it was how long it takes to get used to new experiences coming one after the other. How long it would take for me to remind myself not to let my jaw drop.

Because I was supposed to be the one totally on top of the situation. The one who had it together at all times. How long would it be before I thought *Not* another *C-17 flying into a war zone. Not another rock concert drumming for Shadow. Oh, yawn.*

Once we were backstage on the base in Kabul, I didn't have time to obsess over the drum parts because I was also concentrating on keeping an eye out for potential kidnappers. And I didn't have time to obsess about kidnappers because I had to remember the drum parts.

Although, actually, Colin and I both doubted they'd make their move in Kabul. Folks on USO tours were under the protection of the troops at the base where they performed. So we were surrounded by U.S. military packing heat, as well as my new friend Deet, who was Shadow's regular bodyguard. To my mind, warding off kidnappers was kind of like playing soccer, and I was the goalie. If the ball ever got as far as me, it meant several lines of defense had already failed.

In Kabul, on the base, our lines of defense were mighty. If I were planning to kidnap either Thorne or Talya, I would wait until they were further out, at one of the smaller forward operating bases. Even then, it wouldn't be easy.

At least, that's what I told myself, onstage in Kabul, so that I could relax enough to concentrate on playing the drums.

It was great. All those hours I'd spent at home practicing, fantasizing about what it would be like to be a rock star, didn't come close. Playing the fills, rocking the beat, smiling at Thorne when he smiled at me, being part of the moment, completely surrounded by the music and the moment and the crowd, was heaven.

Afterward, we met lots of the soldiers. They were grateful we'd come. We even took pictures with many of them. I could only imagine years later, them looking at Shadow albums, and looking at me, and wondering who the heck I was. But for the moment, it was a pure adrenaline high.

Until I noticed, after maybe twenty minutes, that Talya was gone.

CHAPTER TEN

Mad Wheels

WHERE COULD TALYA be? Had she been kidnapped already? How could she have been kidnapped already?

If she'd gone off on her own, I would be so mad that I'd call the kidnappers myself and hand her over. Seriously. The girl was trouble.

Trying to remain calm, I walked behind the stage to where the small trailers that served as dressing rooms were parked. The trailer the guys and I had used seemed empty, but I noticed that the door to Talya's was shut.

I stopped.

I knocked.

The door cracked open. Talya's head appeared. "What took you so long?" she asked. She grabbed my arm and pulled me inside.

Before I could say anything, she said, "Okay, Spy Guy, here's the plan."

She was wearing black pants, a turquoise tunic, and a beige headscarf. Her flowing hair was tucked away somehow. She looked like a local.

"This is Jeannie." She pointed behind me, and I turned to see another young woman, probably in her mid-twenties. Jeannie wore a longer tan tunic with paisley print, white pants, and a matching headscarf.

"I've made arrangements to visit one of the local places that my mother was covering on her journalistic beat. It's been okayed and cleared by everybody. Jeannie works there and will take me over. The thing is, since we're trying to be very careful, it can't be a big Shadow outing. I've got to slip out and slip back. The streets of Kabul are probably pretty dangerous for me and Thorne right now, so the fewer people who know I've gone out, the better.

"Thorne is going to stay here and keep the attention on him. But I need a man to go with me. I don't have a man. You're going to have to do."

Obviously, she had never read *How to Win Friends and Influence People.*

Or even *Colt's Common Sense Guidebook.* For the record, Colt's Rule Number 1: If you need someone to do you a favor, don't start by insulting him.

"You're telling me you've gotten permission. From the USO."

"And the Army. The people where we're going know my mom. She might have told them something that would be helpful to us. Let's go. We don't have much time."

"Seriously?"

"Seriously, yes. Captain Roselle will escort us to the car, which is waiting out back. Now, you coming or not?"

Jeannie, who looked nice and on the up-and-up, nodded.

"Okay. I guess."

Domino eight.

That was all it took. They started for the door.

As Talya swept past me, I grabbed her arm. "I'm coming with you this time," I said. "But listen to me. No more surprises. We're on the same team. We plan things together. I'm here to keep you alive. You got that?"

She looked unexpectedly chastened. "This is

important. I couldn't risk anyone saying no or trying to stop me." She gave me what could be interpreted as an apologetic look. It was obviously as much of a "sorry" as I was going to get. I let her go.

Captain Roselle, the female Army captain tasked to escort Shadow around, knocked on the door. "Car's waiting," she said.

And so we wound up in an old Chevy driving the streets of Kabul on a sunny Tuesday afternoon. I sat in front with the male driver, who seemed to be a coworker of Jeannie's. The two women sat in the backseat.

The driver and I didn't talk the whole way. I looked straight ahead, trying to seem blasé. Just a local out on local business. I tried to stay alert but not panic. What if someone knew we'd left the base? What if Jeannie wasn't who she said she was? Was the driver a friend of hers? Or was he an unknown person who'd already kidnapped us, and we just didn't know it yet? Would we end up in an airless basement room, making videos while holding up today's paper? Somehow almost every imagining of how this Afghan trip was going to go in my mind ended up with that scenario.

There were sand-colored guard walls up everywhere, protecting houses and apartment buildings. Minarets dotted the skyscape of the city. Men drove nondescript cars; some were on motor scooters. All the women walking wore head coverings. Some wore scarves and tunics like Talya and Jeannie; others were covered completely by sky-blue burqas. I saw some pigs down one side street, but no children in the parts of town we passed. How could you let your children go out to play when the streets were dangerous at worst, unpredictable at best?

We passed the National Stadium—originally built as a sports arena, but more famous now for the public executions and maimings held by the Taliban. I shuddered.

But just past it, we turned and drove through a gate in a large, fenced-in complex. The moment we parked, Jeannie and Talya were out of the car, Talya chattering happily. I'd never seen her this relaxed and animated— and here we were, in the middle of Kabul. I got out of the car and followed behind, but it was as if she'd forgotten she'd even dragged me along.

In front of us, inside the chain-link fence, sat a huge building. The bottom half was rectangular and painted with blue, red, and black stripes—the Afghan national colors. The top half of the building was a half circle. I followed the women inside, not at all prepared for what I found.

Just inside the door was a large hallway. I could see rooms and a large staircase off to my left. But Talya was making a beeline straight ahead. I followed her through a door and was stunned to find myself at one end of a gigantic indoor skate park.

Talya came over to me. "The woman I've come to talk to will be off a call in a few minutes. In the meantime, I'll wait here."

By "here," she apparently meant across the park. She walked over to where a group of girls, probably ranging from ten to seventeen, were warming up for a skateboard session. Jeannie handed Talya a board and a helmet as she crossed the room. She also pulled on knee and elbow guards.

A girl of about fifteen was leading the warm-up. The dozen or so young women who surrounded her smiled and nodded at the newcomer, but remained focused on what they were doing.

"There aren't many places in Afghanistan where a girl can learn a sport," came Jeannie's voice from beside me. "Skateistan is an official Afghan Olympic training facility. It's run by foreign donations as well as the Olympic ministry here in Afghanistan. About 250 kids skateboard here—and more than half of them are girls. Girls who otherwise might not be allowed to go to school, or even to leave the house."

"They go to school here?" I asked.

"Well, for every hour they skate, they have an hour of classes. But we don't replicate school. We teach leadership, video skills, international relations—things that will be useful that they couldn't learn anywhere else. But we really push every skater to go to school. If they are willing to commit, we will help get them enrolled and get them to classes—neither of which are easy to do."

"Both boys and girls?"

"Both. For sure. If the boys don't learn to see beyond their own war-torn streets, there will always be war. If the girls don't learn a skill, or that there is a wider world that will welcome them, they will be trapped, uneducated, behind the walls of their fathers' or husbands' homes."

I watched as Talya and the girls completed their warm-ups and began to skate. They were mostly similarly dressed—tunics and pants—but they'd replaced their headscarves with helmets. Someone cranked up the music and the serious skating began.

This was obviously not the beginners' group. These girls had some mad skateboarding abilities. I remembered what Jeannie had said about this being a training facility. Obviously.

I remembered that extreme-sports charity show I'd watched a year ago. Here I was, in person, watching Talya Ellis burn up the course.

A young man came up behind us and shouted something to Jeannie, who then walked halfway across the park and signaled to Talya.

Talya came off the floor with a giant grin on her face. She handed back the helmet and skateboard and we both turned to follow Jeannie through the lobby area over to the wide set of stairs.

Upstairs, we passed the classrooms, which were windowed and full of light. Then we came to the main office, where four or five desks were occupied, phones ringing, computers on. In the back of the office wall was a window overlooking the skate floor below.

"Talya!" A woman in her thirties stood from behind one of the desks and walked quickly around to join us. "I'm so glad to meet you! I've heard so much about you and your brother from your mom."

"Thanks so much for letting me come," Talya said. "This place is amazing." Then Talya turned to me. "Mara, this is Colt. He's come along to help me and Thorne."

"Come on," Mara said. "There's a room down the hall where we can talk."

The room Mara took us to was a small kitchen, with a knee-height fridge and a microwave. No one else was there. Mara closed the door and sat down at the square Formica-topped table.

"So, how is your mother?" she asked, smiling at Talya.

"I don't know," Talya replied, and Mara's smile fled immediately.

"What do you mean?"

"We haven't heard from her for nearly two weeks now. I was wondering—hoping, really—that she might have said something to you about where she was going, or if she was investigating something?"

"A couple of weeks? Really? That is odd, especially since she knew you were coming. I can't imagine she wouldn't be here to meet you."

Mara didn't finish the sentence, but it was clear the last part was "if she could."

We all sat there, music filtering up from below, the energetic sound of wheels as percussion.

"Did she say anything about where she was going or stories she was pursuing last time she left?"

"She'd been visiting schools that had been set up

for girls in various cities. Many were operating secretly. There was one she liked and had visited several times that was doing a lot with music. She'd been following the story of a girl at that school. But last time she stopped in, the girl was sick and your mom hadn't been able to see her. She'd offered to get medical help, but they said it wasn't necessary. Your mom did say she was going to check in again soon on the girl. That might not be it at all, but it's the only specific I can remember."

"Which school was it? Do you remember where it is?"

"It was in Kandahar Province, somewhere in the city of Kandahar. I don't remember the name of the school. I'm so sorry."

"We're performing at an Air Force base in Kandahar." I could see the little wheels turning behind Talya's eyes. "Thanks. It's a good lead. Right now, it's our only lead."

"I'm so glad you got to stop in and see the place here. Like I said, I've heard so much about you."

We all stood up. "And, Talya, I know this isn't a cheerful thought, but—if she'd been kidnapped, or if something had happened to her—you likely *would* have heard."

"I guess that's right," the younger woman said. "I'll hold that thought."

The three of us walked together down the wide stairs and back to the waiting vehicle. "So, you skate?" I asked Talya, though I obviously knew the answer.

"Yeah. I'm kind of into extreme sports," she said. "My dad says it's because the whole rock star thing came so easily for me, I feel like I've got to prove myself doing dangerous stuff to get a rush."

"What do you mean, it came so easily? I thought you told me you've practiced every day since you were three."

"There are lots of talented people who have practiced since they were three, Spy Guy," she said. "Most of them are not here."

"When do we go to Kandahar?" I asked.

"Day after tomorrow."

We got into the car after that and didn't talk again as we drove back through Kabul. I knew she was worried sick about her mom.

And I had the sinking feeling I knew where the bad guys might decide to make their move.

CHAPTER ELEVEN

Kandahar

WE TOOK A Chinook helicopter to our final concert at Kandahar Air Field. I had been keeping a list of new life experiences, but was quickly running out of mental paper. Maybe I should keep a list of the stuff I was doing that I'd already done. It would be shorter.

Anyhow, compared to other helicopters we'd been on going to smaller outposts, the Chinook was huge. It easily fit the band and all our equipment; in fact, we could have added a horn section.

The Chinook was very noisy, so we didn't talk much, which gave me time to think. We'd done four more concerts since Talya's side trip to Skateistan, and at every concert and every meet and greet, both she and Thorne had been very pleased to interact with the soldiers and had shown great interest in them. But now, sitting quietly, they both seemed to be lost in their own thoughts and downright worried.

Mara's words about their mom circled in my mind: *If she'd been kidnapped, or if something had happened to her—you likely would have heard.*

It reminded me, not surprisingly, of my own mom and the dinner I'd had with her and Agent Restive the night before I left. We'd gone back to Mom's place, and Colin had gone out to pick up some good local barbecue.

Mom had a condominium with a kickin' view of the Chicago skyline. As the three of us sat around the table, there had been a lot of laughter. It was clear that she and Agent Restive knew each other very well and enjoyed each other's company. Somehow they were able to include me in the conversation like I'd always been around.

As we finished up with some cheesecake, Mom looked at me and said, "Colin told me that you've accepted Mr. Waverly's offer of an active assignment."

My fork was halfway to my mouth. I set it back down. "Yes," I said.

"Colt," she said, "you have to understand that this isn't easy for me. Ever since I was younger than you are now, I've been out in the field, risking my life. Somehow, after your dad died, things changed. It was a lot harder at first. But after I had you . . . even though you weren't physically with me, it was a comfort knowing that you were somewhere safe. That if anything ever happened to me, I had left behind a legacy, something valuable."

I studied the piece of cheesecake on the fork as I tried to frame my emotions into words. "But I've met you now. Everything's changed for me too."

"I know," she said.

"Yesterday, my mom was this nice, quiet person who lived at home in Springfield. But now you're my mom. And, well, I've got something at stake too. How am I supposed to live like nothing's going on when you're out there, risking your life? 'Cause now there would be a huge hole if *you* were suddenly gone."

Amber Coltrane reached across the table and covered my hand with hers.

"I know," she said. "So as hard as it is, I guess we've both got to understand who the other one is. We're both Active, and that's cool. In fact, very cool. It's something we share. And, if something happens to one of us, we'll be very sad. But we'll also be very proud."

She smiled at me.

I said, "Cool." And I had meant it.

Now I figured that Talya and Thorne, the rock stars, and their journalist parents, must have come to the same kind of agreement, whether tacit or spoken. And I understood, perhaps too well, the nagging fear that the day of being sad/proud might be coming too quickly for any of us.

Kandahar Air Field was like a little city. The concert was in the "town square," a large, open field of dust surrounded by American fast-food restaurants and other vendors. In fact, if you didn't pay attention to the heat and the dust—and the fact that the audience all wore matching outfits—it could have been an open-air concert just about anywhere. When Thorne hit the first notes of their latest hit song and I came in behind him on drums, the kind of mass audience cheer went up that I'm sure greeted the band everywhere. For a moment I was bummed that this was my last concert as part of Shadow.

But it only lasted a second. This was Kandahar, Afghanistan, and I was onstage with my favorite band.

I did my best to play the drums and watch the crowd at the same time. Mostly, movement in the crowd had to do with people getting stuff from the Pizza Hut pickup window. And not everyone was military; there were guys in chinos and polos, and even some local men in tunics and women wearing headscarves.

We'd been playing for a while when I noticed a woman in a green tunic and an ivory headscarf who had slipped in over to the side. She'd come in toward the back, but was unobtrusively working her way forward. Most of her face was covered.

She seemed to be enjoying the concert, but she also seemed distracted.

I wondered if I had noticed her because she wasn't military; I didn't want to feel like I was profiling the locals or anything. But she was purposefully making her way closer and closer to the stage.

Then I noticed that every once in a while she'd glance across to the other side of the crowd. I followed her line of vision and eventually noticed a man, a local in civilian clothes, also making his way forward, little by little. The two glanced at each other, but only very rarely.

Why should it matter? I wondered. Lots of people, in uniform and out, were jostling for a better spot in the crowd, closer to the stage. But there seemed to be an underlying sense of purpose to these two.

Thorne started the next tune. This one had been new to me, with a pretty tricky drum groove, and I got pulled back into the music. When I looked back again, toward the end of the song, the woman and man were gone.

Afterward, we did a meet and greet, as we'd done after each concert. Darrell, the keyboardist, always joined them front and center, and usually people wanted my autograph too, even though many of them knew who Rip Ettinger was, and that I was not him.

This time, though, I extricated myself from the press around the band and headed for Deek, the bodyguard. I told him what I'd seen and described what the woman and man were wearing. He nodded but didn't say anything. I couldn't tell how seriously he took what I was saying. And maybe it wasn't serious.

Once again, I got pulled forward to sign people's CDs. I still felt like a fraud, but part of me wished I could get a CD myself, signed by the whole band—including me. No one at home would believe it. When I was old and in a retirement village, I would get a kick out of looking at it.

I caught Thorne's eye, and we smiled at each other. Shelly, the USO organizer who traveled with us, gave the wrap-up sign. There was still a group of soldiers—nearly all handsome young men—gathered around Talya. There always were.

As we walked over to politely extricate Talya, I saw her. The woman who had been in the crowd. She'd been waiting beyond the signing area, just out of sight. The man, who was at least a head taller than she was, stood behind her. I gasped, and I swear my heart stopped cold, missing a couple of beats.

You know how in the movies, when the big moment comes, things move into slow motion? That's exactly how those next moments felt. I could see each movement that the woman made, as she quickly and quietly moved toward Thorne. She was behind him, so he couldn't see her coming. There was this intensity of purpose in her eyes that scared the living daylights out of me.

I clearly saw the embroidered flower design on her ivory-colored headscarf as I made the leap to put myself between her and Thorne. I saw the look of confusion on Thorne's face as I sailed past him, and the surprise in the woman's eyes as I knocked into her and we both went flying onto the ground. And I remembered the shape of her face, and the nagging thought that it looked slightly familiar to me, as I landed on top of her with an *oof* of expelled air.

Then Thorne was above us and Talya was running over. There were tears in her eyes as she flung herself onto the ground and cried out, "Mom!"

CHAPTER TWELVE

Visit

So that's how I met Sophie Ellis. After Thorne and Talya got her up, I wanted to go straight back to school and quietly study the countries bordering the Mediterranean. I was mortified. Certainly everyone could tell this was my first—and, probably, my last—active assignment.

But once on her feet, Mrs. Ellis turned to me and said, "Wow, you've got world-class security. Well done, young man."

It was nice of her. I still wanted to die.

She quickly introduced the other man I'd noticed

as Rachman, her driver. Then Sophie, Talya, and Thorne headed back to the trailer they'd been given as a dressing room. What was my part in this? I wasn't sure. But since Rachman followed them inside, I did too. Deek stayed outside. He punched my shoulder as I walked by. I couldn't tell if he was more proud or amused.

Once inside, Sophie took off her headscarf and shook out her blondish hair, which now had streaks of white, and not just from the dust. Thorne got to her first and scooped her into a giant bear hug, easily lifting her off the ground and twirling her around. "Mom!" he said, "Thank God! Thank God. And this is our last concert. Now we can all get out of here and go home!"

When he set her down, she looked up at him, still holding his arms, and said, "And a great concert it was! I loved what you did with the bridge in 'Turpentine.'"

He lit up.

Talya hugged her next and didn't let go. It sort of seemed like she was trying not to cry. "I'm so glad you're safe!" the daughter said as she finally pulled away.

"Thank God you're safe also," said Sophie.

"So, what's been going on?" asked Thorne. Talya

passed out bottles of water to each of us from the stash that had been left inside the door.

"Who's been threatening you—and us?" asked Talya. "Insurgents? The Taliban?"

Sophie sank down onto a small sofa. "I'm afraid it's trickier than that," she answered. "I've crossed some down-and-dirty opportunists. It's hard to believe there are people who will come into a difficult situation and try to profit from it, but they're everywhere. Always have been, likely always will be."

"What's the situation?" asked Thorne. "How have you crossed them?"

"I don't think I have—yet. I think they're trying to scare me off before I find out what's going on. There's a girls' school here that seems to be doing good things. Teaching the girls both school subjects and art and music. It's well hidden along some back alleyways in the outskirts of the city, and I did my best to visit whenever I was here in Kandahar. But something's changed.

"There's a family I've known here for many years, under different regimes. Fourteen years ago, they named a daughter after me. Sophie—AnaSophia, actually. They sent her to this school, which is how I found out about it. AnaSophia is a lovely girl. She's shy at first, but underneath she has one of those sparkly personalities. As well as a great singing voice.

"But last time I visited, the couple who ran the school were not at all welcoming. They asked me not to return because they were afraid I might bring unwanted attention, which I understand. But when I asked to see AnaSophia to say good-bye, they refused to let me see her and abruptly threw us out. I'm very concerned.

"That night I got a threatening text from a blocked cell number. It said if I cared about the girls, I was never to go back. That if I did, my own children wouldn't leave Afghanistan alive. Which meant they knew you were coming here."

"Mom," Thorne said, "you don't know for sure that anything is wrong. Sure, you got a threatening text, but maybe they're scared of the local clerics. It's an overreaction, but maybe they were feeling threatened. You're here now, and we're all together. We're leaving in the morning. Come with us. Please."

There was this look in Sophie Ellis's eyes. I don't know how to describe it, except maybe peaceful steel. Like she wasn't mad at Thorne for suggesting that, but it wasn't going to happen.

"Maybe," she said. "Maybe."

"Maybe, if what?" Thorne asked. He was getting perturbed. Apparently he'd seen the peaceful-steel look before.

"If I can get this cleared up tonight. Now that I know you're here, and safe, I can do a little pushing."

"Pushing? Who? How?" His voice was rising.

"Just let me make sure nothing terrible is happening and that AnaSophia is all right."

"How are you going to do that?"

"I want to visit her parents, to see if they've heard from her, or if maybe she's home and the school didn't tell me for some reason. If they have any idea what's going on. But if they haven't heard from her, I'll go back to the school."

"You'll go back and what?"

"Find her."

"How will you do that?" Thorne was not happy.

His mother just looked at him and smiled. I had a feeling my own mother had that same expression in her arsenal. If I had to translate, I'd go with *Sheer force of will gets many things done.*

"No," said Thorne.

"If that's what it will take to get you to leave with us, let's go," said Talya.

Everyone turned to look at her.

145

"To AnaSophia's house. Let's go. Let's see if she's there."

"But we're here with the USO. They'll never let us off the base."

This time both women turned and looked at Thorne. If I hadn't been to Skateistan, I would have agreed with him.

Sheer force of will, indeed.

That quickly, it was decided. Talya and Thorne reluctantly went to oversee the packing up of their equipment, and Mrs. Ellis prepared to visit the commander of the base. But as she and Rachman prepared to follow the teenagers out the door, their mom stopped and turned to me. "So you're a friend of Mr. Waverly's?" she asked.

The question caught me off guard. "Yes, ma'am," I said. It felt slightly like I was admitting to being in Alcoholics Anonymous or something. Like there was a secret handshake and we both knew it.

"Good," she said, looking me up and down. "Well chosen. And they sent us a drummer! What's your name?"

"Colt," I said.

"Well, Colt, thanks for looking out for my kids. I haven't officially introduced you to Rachman, my driver.

146

He is actually a journalist himself, though we can't say so anymore. We are hopeful that will change. In any case, you'll come with us?"

Domino nine.

"Yes, ma'am," I said. Technically, I was here to protect Thorne and Talya. If Talya went, keeping her safe was still the first objective.

"Great. I think you'd best change into a better version of local clothes while I go and speak to Commander Roberts."

Rachman gave me a slight bow, and I followed him back outside.

CHAPTER THIRTEEN

Behind the Walls

TURNS OUT IT'S not that easy to get off a military base in a war zone, even with a note from your mother. Mrs. Ellis obviously knew the base commander; her job as a journalist had brought her on and off the base in the past.

"We're cleared to go," she said. She lowered her voice. "Now."

It had been decided that Thorne would stay and help pack up everything so we'd all be ready to leave with the USO the next day. Talya changed back into the same outfit she'd worn to visit Skateistan. She looked very much like a local.

As did I. Rachman had loaned me a pair of loose white trousers, with a white shirt and a dark vest. The look was completed with a rounded white cap. If my hair was slightly darker (and if the clothing was a size smaller), I would have totally felt like I belonged here.

Mrs. Ellis led us quickly to their vehicle. Once there, I stopped dead in my tracks. It had three wheels, an enclosed two-passenger cab, and an open truck bed in the back. It looked like a cross between a golf cart and a scooter, the sort of thing traffic cops rode around in giving out parking tickets. Sophie and Talya piled into the back, and I saw both women pulling some sort of garment over their heads. Rachman nodded me to the passenger seat of the cab. Even before I had both feet inside, he'd started the engine and taken off.

I saw Thorne in the rearview mirror, looking unhappy.

I wondered why we were taking off like a bat out of hell. As we pulled through the exit gate and Rachman talked to the young guard, I saw a huge black armored vehicle pull up next to Thorne, a quarter mile behind us.

"Who's talking to Thorne?" I asked.

"That's the car Commander Roberts arranged for us," Rachman answered. "It's fully up-armored and comes with armed guards as standard equipment."

"And we left without it?" I was slightly aghast.

"No one in Kandahar would tell us a damn thing if we pulled up in that car," he said.

And with that answer, I realized the occupants of this car cared more about finding answers than staying safe.

I wish I'd called Colin.

We pulled out into the streets. "This doesn't seem very sturdy," I said. "I mean, if we hit an IED or something."

"These days, they're not using improvised explosive devices as much as landmines. I'll still watch out for them, but you've got to be extra careful when you step out of the car."

"Oh. Thanks."

I glanced back through the small rectangular window behind me. Both Talya and Mrs. Thorne were gone— replaced by two anonymous females in full burqa. I couldn't tell who was in the brown and who was in the blue. They were covered from head to toe, with a small screen woven over the place where their eyes would be.

"Is that really necessary?" I asked.

"You never know," said Rachman. "You never know in Kandahar. This city has seen so much turnover in its history, you must always expect the worst. Kandahar was the birthplace of the Taliban. So it's best to be careful. In fact, if we are stopped, we speak only Pashto. You must not speak at all."

Great.

We were not stopped. Somewhere along the way, my fascination with the local landscape overcame my trepidation—really, when would I see the streets of Kandahar again in person? We drove through the busier streets of town, passing many men out on bicycles, in old cars, and in carts like ours. Buildings were sand colored or white, except those with splashes of color. The downtown looked like it had been interesting and inviting in decades not completely forgotten. Tiny shops were tucked in beside larger buildings painted in blues and greens.

Then the shops were behind us, and we were driving along smaller streets and alleyways. I realized that I had calmed down. How could you live here and worry every second about going over a mine? You'd die of a heart attack. If it happened, it happened.

We reached a residential area. At least I assumed it was—you couldn't actually see houses behind the tall walls surrounding them. Rachman came to a stop in front of one.

"Don't talk," was all he said as he got out.

"Should I stay here in the car?" I asked.

"Not a good idea."

I got out my side. We went back and helped the women out. Rachman then led the way up the walk and through an iron gate in a rounded doorway. From there, we walked through a walled garden up to the door of the house. Neither woman spoke as he rang the bell.

There was a rectangular grillwork just at eye level, and within minutes, a piece of wood slid back behind it. Rachman said something in Pashto, and the wooden panel slid back again. Another couple of moments, and the door opened.

Inside, we were greeted by much cooler air. The women followed behind us. A young man dressed much the same as I invited us down the steps into the sunken living room. He said something to which Rachman responded; the young man gave a small bow and left up the hall.

It wasn't long before two women appeared, carrying a large tray with coffee and cups. We were all seated on the carpeted floor and served. Then the man of the house appeared—AnaSophia's father, I presumed—sat down, and launched into a lengthy discussion with Rachman. The men shared a smoke and laughed heartily. Thankfully, I was not expected to join in. All the women sat silently through this whole meeting.

Then AnaSophia's name was mentioned by her father. Rachman asked something, speaking in serious tones. The father replied, also sounding concerned, but not overly so. They continued their conversation, but within a few minutes, the father had his arm around Rachman's shoulders, and both men were smiling. It was clear that AnaSophia's father was not descending to our level of worry.

To me, this boded well for the missing girl. Surely her own father would be the one to take up the investigation if something wasn't right.

The two men shook hands, and the father headed back up the hall.

Everyone else filed out behind him. The younger man who had originally met us moved toward the outside door and we followed. As Rachman and I stepped back out into the heat of the day, one of the women of the family hurried back into the living room to pick up something she'd left behind. As she did, she paused just long enough to mutter something to Mrs. Ellis, audible only to her. The two women clasped hands for a brief moment and then headed in separate directions.

Once we were all in the courtyard, the door shut firmly behind us.

Rachman had been heading toward the street door,

but now that we were alone, he stopped in the middle of the courtyard.

Mrs. Ellis and Talya came up beside him. The older woman lifted back the front part of the veil from her burqa, so Talya did the same.

"What did she say?" Talya asked.

"She asked us not to look for AnaSophia any further. She said they'd paid a good sum of money to the school to get AnaSophia out of the country. She's going to be taken to a host family, given a good education, and have an advantageous marriage arranged."

To me, this sounded like wonderful news. There didn't seem to be much of a future for a bright young girl here in this war-torn city, where, even without the Taliban in control, opportunities for females seemed strictly limited.

But the looks that were passing between Rachman and Mrs. Ellis were anything but comforting. "It sounds bad," said Mrs. Ellis.

"Very bad," agreed our driver.

"What's bad about it?" I asked. "Getting out of Kandahar seems like a fantastic idea, for her and for us."

"We've had cause to distrust the people who are running the school for a while now," said Mrs. Ellis.

"Once those girls leave Kandahar, there's no way to hold anyone accountable for what happens to them. Get them out to where? Or, worse, to *whom*?"

The four of us stood, looking at each other. Once we left the relative privacy of that courtyard, we would not be able to have any sort of lengthy public conversation. So where we were to go, what would happen next, would have to be decided right here and now.

The school's owners had warned Mrs. Ellis not to come back. The girl's mother had told us to leave well enough alone. Something bad could happen to the girls once they were out of Afghanistan. But maybe the promises that had been made would be kept. What could we do? Hide outside the school and wait for a bunch of girls to go by and follow them?

There was only one possible course of action: head back to the airfield, get the heck out of there, and hope and pray for the best for the schoolgirls.

"I guess it's up to me," said Talya.

"How so?" Mrs. Ellis asked.

"Pay to get me inside the school. I'll talk to AnaSophia. I'll—I'll figure out how to track her somehow, in case things do go bad. Then I'll get out."

"They're leaving very soon," said Mrs. Ellis.

"Then we'd better get over there," said Talya.

I waited for Talya's mother to explain that this was a terrible idea; that Talya could end up in the hands either of human traffickers, if she stayed in the school, or insurgents, if she went with the girls when they left. Either way would be unacceptably dangerous.

And would we really be helping? Was getting AnaSophia away from the school and leaving her here in Kandahar, where girls had no education and no hope, a happy ending?

On the other hand, was marching her across the border into Iran or Pakistan, where the girls could be apprehended by insurgents anywhere along the way, a happy ending?

So many things could go wrong, and I could see very little that could go right.

I waited for Mrs. Ellis to explain this to her daughter.

Instead, she said to Rachman, "You've heard Talya speak Pashto. How's her accent?"

"Passable," he said. "If she doesn't talk too much."

A smug little smile spread across Talya's face.

Mrs. Ellis then turned to me. "What have you got?" she asked. "I mean, in the way of tracking devices—or anything that would be helpful."

I stared at her. "Doesn't this seem completely dangerous to you? If Talya is kidnapped, it becomes an international incident," I argued. "And AnaSophia is only one girl."

Have you ever said something and wished you could have the words back the instant they left your mouth? That's exactly how I felt on that hot afternoon.

"Only one girl?" asked Mrs. Ellis.

"Only one girl?" asked Talya. "And what makes AnaSophia's life any less important than mine?"

I thought I saw an ounce of sympathy in Rachman's eyes, but he was the only one.

"I didn't mean . . . ," I started. "Of course she's important. Everyone's important. I'm just not seeing a good way out of this."

Oh, man. I was the wrong guy for this job. My first assignment I should be following Talya to a mall or something, not making life-and-death decisions in a dusty courtyard in Afghanistan. My mission was to keep Talya safe, and yet here we stood, outside the perimeter of the Air Force base, with her about to go undercover in a highly volatile situation.

Yes, my mission was to keep Talya safe and get her home. But the ultimate mission, as taught by our school, was to make the world a better place.

Human trafficking is a really big problem. Children

are sold every day, into armies or the sex trade or whatever. If that was happening here, wasn't it my job to try to stop it?

But I'd also been taught that successful missions depended on planning and seeing a clear way to a successful resolution, not flying by the seat of your pants and hoping for the best.

Domino ten.

I dug my hand into my pocket and pulled out the two tracking disks that I'd been given back at headquarters. "These are tracking devices," I said.

"One for Talya and one for AnaSophia," said Mrs. Ellis. "Anything else?"

Obviously, I couldn't part with my watch; it wouldn't work for anybody else anyway.

Hesitantly, I withdrew my phone from my pocket. "This will connect you to me," I said. "And if you can get a photo of the people running the school, and send it along"—I demonstrated—"we might be able to ID them and know who we're dealing with."

Sophie Ellis smiled, like I wasn't a total lost cause.

Talya took the phone and started playing with it. "So we're doing this thing?" she asked.

"You get in. You find AnaSophia. You give her the disk or plant it on her. You get out," said the mom. Then she turned to Rachman. "You're okay doing this?" she asked. "They know me. They don't want me back, and they certainly don't want a girl there planted by me."

"I can do it," he said.

"How much do you think they'll want?" she asked. "In dollars."

"We'll have to find out. Ten thousand?"

"Okay. Come on, we need to leave this house before we cause any suspicion."

CHAPTER FOURTEEN

Still Kandahar

I GOT BACK in on my side of the car and we rode in silence through the back streets. There were no shops in these neighborhoods; in fact, you were more likely to see goats or dogs wandering around. We finally stopped by the entrance to an alleyway. Rachman got out, turned around, and lifted up the driver's seat. From underneath, he took out what seemed to be a bundle of cash. It disappeared into the waistband of his pants before he stood up.

"I stay here?" I asked.

"Yes. We may need you later, so it's helpful that they don't see you now."

They may need me later. Of course they might.

Rachman stepped gingerly around our little scooter, his eyes sweeping the ground for any signs of explosives as he walked to the back of the scooter and helped Talya down. Together, they slid silently down the deserted alleyway in front of us.

If only the president of her record label could see her now, I thought.

The next half an hour sitting in the cab of that scooter seemed like the longest of my life. I was a sitting duck. If anyone came along, I couldn't even talk to them. Mrs. Ellis had lain down in the back of the cart so that from a distance you couldn't tell there was a woman in the car.

When Rachman finally returned, he was alone.

He silently got back into the scooter and we took off. We didn't talk.

We drove to another section of town, where things were in better repair and there were more people on the streets. We came to a street of freestanding houses, each encircled by a gigantic wall. Rachman pulled up to a gate, put a code into a box, and the gate opened. It slid shut quickly behind us. Together we went inside.

The house was shared by several foreign aid workers.

They gathered at the table to hear about the concert—but the story Rachman told sobered them immediately.

It had taken a lot of money to get the owners of the school to take Talya. He'd told them friends had sent him and his daughter and had told him the price to get her out of the country. They said there was a surcharge because they were leaving soon and would have to pay an exorbitant amount to get Talya's documents. He'd finally given them the equivalent of twelve thousand dollars cash. He asked when they were leaving, but got no answer other than "Soon."

As we were sitting at the table talking, my watch bipped. We all jumped, and I hit the button to see what had come in.

I'd gotten a message from Talya.

It was a voice message converted to text: "Never alone. Leaving soon. Will let you know."

Mrs. Ellis looked at Rachman. "Did they tell you when they were leaving?"

"They said within a day or two."

"What's our best guess as to how they're getting the girls out?"

"Through the desert, across the border into either Iran or Pakistan," said one of the aid workers. "But if they are, they will likely have paid for some sort of armed protection. I don't know how you'll get this other girl away from them, even if you . . . *after* you get Talya back."

Rachman said calmly, "In the morning, as soon as Talya can put a trace on AnaSophia—and maybe get a photo of the man in charge—we'll get her out. I'll say her mom has had a change of heart and can't bear to have her go."

"That might be the most logical story," said Rachman. "I think now our best course is to get some rest so we're ready to pick up and go," said Rachman.

We had a simple dinner, and they showed me to a small guest room with a single bed against one wall. I went in and shut the door.

This seemed like the perfect time to check in with Colin.

I called him on my watch phone and described all that had happened. I tried not to sound like an idiot, but I felt like one, completely out of control of the situation. He was a top agent, the best, and more than anything I wanted him to think well of me. But after describing where I was and why, I heard myself saying, "I'm sorry, Colin, I know I was sent here to protect Thorne and Talya and keep them safely on the base. I just didn't know how to make her stay, especially with her mother wanting her to go. I feel like I've failed, like things are out of my control. I'm sorry! I'm handling it all wrong. I don't know what to do."

Unexpectedly, he laughed.

"Colt, listen. You are inexperienced. Assignments aren't like roller coasters with a car that goes up and down but stays on the tracks. They're situations involving human beings, decisions, and constantly moving pieces. The assignment you're given is seldom the assignment you end up on. But when there's a course of action before you, you first decide if it's the best course, given the circumstances. Then you fully commit. On assignments, there is no time for dithering. You review, you decide, you act. You don't keep looking back, two forks in the road ago, thinking, 'What the hell happened?' Only, 'What's the best course of action, given the current circumstances?'"

There was a moment of silence while I processed this.

"So. What is your best course of action, given the circumstances?"

"I guess . . . to see how this plays out and try to get Talya back and safely home."

"And what about AnaSophia?"

"She . . . wasn't part of my assignment." I didn't know if I was allowed to add her to my current plans or not.

"Sophie Ellis and Talya seem to think her safety is a worthy goal. What do you think?"

"Yes. Sure?"

"Well, then. Getting Talya back is your original, and current, objective. We'll add AnaSophia's safety as a secondary objective, and finding out what's really going on with those girls is mixed in there. Make sense?"

"Yes."

"Good. Let's hope Talya can get a photo of the man running the operation and get out of there. Let's hope you're all back on base, heading home, tomorrow."

It was a relief to hear that things happen, objectives change, and I wasn't fired before I finished my first assignment.

"Colin?"

"Yes?"

"Is Agent Coltrane—Mom, I mean—following what's going on?"

"No one who isn't on the team of an assignment knows what's going on. She knows you're all right."

"Okay. Thanks."

"Get some rest. Tomorrow will be an interesting day."

Understatement, of course. Understatement.

CHAPTER FIFTEEN

Not Still Kandahar

AN INSISTENT BUZZING pulled me from a sound sleep. It took me a few seconds even after I opened my eyes, to figure out where I was—in Kandahar, Afghanistan—that dawn was breaking, and that I was getting a message on my watch.

It was a text from Talya. It said, "Good news: got a photo. Bad news: heading for airport."

Holy shi . . . cow! *Holy cow!*

I leapt to my feet and steadied myself as my head cleared. Then I went running down the hall to Mrs. Ellis's room.

She woke with a start with my first knock. She was sleeping in her clothes, as we all had been. She swung her legs over the side of the bed. "What is it? What have you heard?"

"They're not escaping through the desert," I said. "They're heading for the airport."

"Now?"

"Yes."

"Let me see."

I pulled the text back up on my wrist and showed her the watch.

"Let me get Rachman," she said.

It was only then that I took the time to open the photo Talya had sent. It was a side view of a man wearing a white shirt, obviously the head of the school. He was slightly turned away, but it was all we had.

I forwarded it for facial recognition.

Then I called Colin.

"They're heading for the airport," I said. "I'm not sure how I'm going to get Talya away from them, or even if she's ready to come."

There was a pause. "So, you're all going to have to follow her to the airport," Colin said.

"Yes."

"And the people from the school could recognize

Sophie Ellis or the man, Rachman, that she's working with?"

"Well, yeah. I guess."

"Then, if worst comes to worst, if they're using a commercial flight, you might have to be the one to board with them. Did you bring your carry-on bag?" Colin asked.

"Yes."

"Good. Use the flip knife from your watch to cut open the stitching on the inside top."

I grabbed the bag and looked inside. There was a sewn hem where the inner and outer pieces of fabric met. I took off my watch, opened the small blade, and gingerly cut through the stitching until I could reach my hand down in between the pieces of cloth. I pulled out two things—a passport and a flat version of a wallet.

The passport was Canadian. I flipped it open. It was my photo, but it said my name was Colton Taylor. The wallet had a Canadian and an international driver's license that said the same thing. It also said I was eighteen. And there were two credit cards.

"Did you find the items?" he asked.

"Yes."

"If you need to purchase a ticket to board that plane, this is what you use. Where is your current passport?"

"In the bag," I answered.

"In the bag, you also have a small hardback novel, do you not?"

"Yes."

"The back cover has a place you can put your current passport for safekeeping; it won't show up on any scanners. Run your fingers along the side of the book and see if you can find it."

I took off the book jacket and found the place to hide my passport; I did that.

Colin spoke again. "We couldn't get facial recognition from the photo," he said. "That means whomever she's with right now isn't known to us. He could be the mastermind, or he could be a messenger delivering the girls to someone we do know. Continue with caution, Colt."

"Okay," I said and signed off.

As I did, both Mrs. Ellis and Rachman appeared at my open door.

"Anything more?" she asked. "Has she said where they're flying?"

I shook my head.

Rachman had been downstairs at the table, online. "There are passenger flights to only three places from Kandahar Airport today: Kabul, Karachi, and Dubai."

"They could certainly get anywhere in the world from Dubai," Rachman said. "But, if they have people in place, they could be met in Karachi and effectively disappear."

I still entertained hope that by going to the airport, which was adjacent to the military base, we could somehow get Talya away from these people and be flying home by military transport later today.

"Do we grab her?" I asked.

"The airport is wall-to-wall guards and rifles," said Rachman. "It seems unlikely that we could even if she wanted to be grabbed."

Up to this point, we hadn't sent any messages to her because we didn't want her to get caught with them. But now there was no other choice. "Shall we grab you?" I asked, and it was translated to text.

It was a while before the reply: "No."

"Where are you going?"

"Will try to find out."

We went outside and got into an old-model car, which the journalists shared among themselves. It was an actual car, with a roof and four wheels and everything. Still, it was Rachman and me in the front seat and Mrs. Ellis in the back. The front gate rolled open. We headed for the airport, which was ten miles south of Kandahar. The Kandahar Airport was built in the 1960s by the Americans, and it must have looked really cool and "space age" back then. Although it has since been banged up through several wars, the nine arches that make the front of the building now stood shimmering in the heat. A long walkway to the building was covered by a half circle. There was hardly a straight line to be seen.

"Sophie, you know that neither of us can come to the civilian part of the airport," Rachman said. "The head of the school would recognize either of us; many people would. The boy will have to fend for himself."

Sophie reluctantly agreed this was so. "We still don't know where they're going. Perhaps you can tell from the gate they're heading for. If not, my money is on Dubai. Good luck, Colt. God be with you."

My adrenaline surged. I could practically feel the blood pulsing through my veins as I got out of the car. *Domino eleven.*

I carried my bag and was under instructions to check it, so I wouldn't seem like a terrorist who walked on at the last minute without checking any bags. Nothing important was in the bag, only clothes the other journalists had donated to the cause, since I might have to ditch it in order to follow the girls when they landed.

Colt Shore was scared to death. So I had no other choice. I got out of the car as Colton Taylor, the Canadian version of myself. Somehow, this Colton was braver than I was. He wasn't afraid to hurry across the walkway and get in line at the ticket counter.

Inside, the civilian part of the terminal was small enough that the passengers for both upcoming flights, including the group of thirteen girls, were not hard to spot. The flights had been announced, and everyone was heading through security. I found the ticket counter for Aero Airlines. There were three men in front of me. When I was nearly to the counter, my watch vibrated slightly. I held my arm up as if I was squinting at the time and hit the button.

Talya had apparently finally been handed her boarding pass to get through security. She'd snapped a photo of it. She was heading for Dubai.

Then two important things happened simultaneously: I bought my ticket without anyone stopping me or arresting me or even pulling me aside for extra security because I was jumping on the plane at the last minute.

And Talya somehow got her phone into the bin and through security without the adults traveling with her noticing.

I went through security myself and headed toward

the gate area where the plane for Dubai was boarding. The girls were already there, herded by two men and one woman. The man Talya had sent a photo of earlier was clearly in charge. Each girl wore an embroidered tunic with a contrasting headscarf; Talya's tunic was green, her headscarf ivory. They kept together and didn't look at anyone else. They seldom spoke to each other. It felt shocking to see Talya as a member of the group. It was if she was no longer Talya at all.

Something sank in the pit of my stomach as the girls all headed for the boarding tunnel. I was leaving every hope of returning to the base, or even to Mrs. Ellis and Rachman, behind. It was becoming a solo mission, at least until Colin could hook me up with someone, wherever we ended up. But in transit, it was just me.

How could this be? I was Classroom Guy, not Agent Guy. I was not Jonny "Baad" Kryder. I was Colt "Boring" Shore.

No. I was Colton Taylor. In that moment, I made a decision. I *was* Colton Taylor. And that braver, more capable version was inside me, available to me. From now to the end of this crazy adventure, I would be Colton Taylor. I would think and act like him.

When I got home, Colton Shore could have a heart attack about it if he so chose.

I grabbed my carry-on and boarded the plane.

After takeoff, I didn't even look down at the trailer on the adjacent Coalition Air Base where all my normal stuff and my drumsticks waited for the other Colton, far below.

The girls were all seated together in the back of the center section. My seat was an aisle seat several rows in front of them. None of them could get to the front of the plane without my seeing them; in fact, I could monitor them out of the corner of my eye. Not that they were doing anything. They all seemed very low energy, which was odd since probably most of them hadn't ever been out of Afghanistan, let alone on an international flight. Many of them dozed. One of their handlers was seated in each row. What else could they do?

My job was to stay unobtrusive enough that they wouldn't notice I was following them once we got off the flight.

But where would we go once we landed in Dubai? I didn't exactly know my way around the city. Or would they continue onto another flight? And if so, how could I possibly get ticketed in time to follow them?

As we got close to landing, a flight attendant came on and gave the weather report for Dubai in four languages. It was the same in all: sunny and hot.

Shortly thereafter, several of the girls, including Talya, got up to use the restrooms in the back of the cabin. The female chaperone followed them.

As soon as Talya was alone in the restroom, a new text popped up on my watch. It was a snap of the boarding pass for their next flight. To Munich.

Germany. Colt Shore would have taken time to think *Oh, good Lord.* Colton Taylor simply forwarded it to headquarters in less time than it would have taken to actually check the time.

As we were landing, I got the response: "You're ticketed on the same flight. Go to the Lufthansa service counter or use your credit card at one of Lufthansa's self-ticketing kiosks to get your boarding pass."

The Dubai Airport was a billion-dollar marvel. From the air, it looked like someone had broken off a gigantic airplane wing and put it on the ground. It was surrounded by planes at their gates. In the distance, the sleek, modern, tall city rose from the former desert.

I deplaned quickly and disappeared into the crowd. The brand-new terminal was jaw-dropping. All the surfaces, including the walls, floors, and moving sidewalks, were white and glowing. There were fountains and palm trees. And everything was rounded and curved. It made the U.S. airports I'd seen look like concrete boxes.

On the way to the next gate, I passed the Lufthansa service desk, and it did indeed have a self-service machine, so I ran my credit card through and a boarding pass was spit out.

I went ahead and staked out a vantage point at a food stand behind the gate and was certain they didn't see me when they arrived.

It wasn't until the flight began to board that I looked at my boarding pass and discovered my seat was in first class.

It made sense. I let the girls board—they were again toward the back of the plane, and therefore in the first group called. I didn't board until final call and went straight to my first-class seat. There was virtually no way they could have seen me.

I hoped Talya wasn't worried.

I settled into my seat and pretended I flew first-class from Dubai every Friday. Then the first-class flight attendant asked what I'd like for my first course. And I decided to stop worrying, at least for the next four and a half hours.

CHAPTER SIXTEEN

Landing

IN THE DISTANCE, I heard drumming. Really good drumming. It started with several great riffs and settled into a steady beat. I recognized it as "Walking Tour," one of Shadow's songs that I hadn't yet been able to nail because the drum part was so virtuoso.

I turned around, surprised to find myself back home in Springfield. I followed the music back toward my bedroom. As I got closer, it became clear someone was playing the song on my own drum set.

Curious, I opened my bedroom door. And there, playing the drums, was my brother—I mean my dad. Dix. He looked up at me and smiled. "Nice drum set," he said. "Never had one when this was my room."

"Nice drumming," I replied.

"I wish I could have met you," he said. He stopped playing and quieted the cymbals.

"Your picture is everywhere," I said.

"Not the same."

"No."

"My mom said all the girls liked you."

"I'm assuming it's the hair." He looked at me then, really looked at me, and said, "I hope the folks are treating you okay. They're good parents, but the whole meat-and-potatoes thing used to make me crazy."

"Me too! I mean, it's okay, but not every meal."

I couldn't believe I was having this conversation. Except that as I thought that, Dix started fading. Like he was less there.

"You want to know the real secret to making the girls swoon over you?"

"Actually, girls are giving me nothing but grief at the moment, but okay."

He smiled. "Get killed on assignment. Saving someone else. Worked with your mom."

His words hit me hard.

"Oh, and with the bridge on the song . . . it's all in remembering that fourth stroke." He played it easily, and then he was gone.

I woke up with a start. As my head cleared, I realized my watch was vibrating.

I was still on the plane. I must have fallen asleep after the meal. I was curled up in this seat/bed/pod thing in first class.

Oh. The watch.

First, I glanced at the time but realized it didn't matter because I wasn't sure exactly where it was that time. Kandahar? Dubai? When had I last reset it?

I glanced around, but there was no one near enough to me to observe what I was doing. I hit the button twice, and the new text message came up. "148215," it said, which meant, "Are you there and free to communicate?" I said, "229713," all clear. I stretched and stood up, casting off the final mantle of sleep. I went into the restroom, locked the door, and said, "Go ahead."

The video screen button flashed, and I hit "allow."

Colin appeared, smiling, on the screen. "Hi, Colt. Nice work. You've managed to keep your cool through some tight spots. Now you need to get Talya out and to a safe house. You'll be landing in Germany shortly. I'm going to put on Reese, who oversees operations in

Europe. He'll tell you what arrangements have been made. Okay?"

"Okay."

I shook the last remnants of sleep from my head. Just the words "safe house" and "Europe" had a happy sound to them.

"Hello," said a man on the screen. He had black hair in a buzz cut, a large nose, and serious gray eyes. "Reese here. You'll be landing in Munich shortly. You need to take your package and get out."

"I'd love to," I said, nodding.

"There's a car waiting in the airport car park. We'll text you the make, model, and license number. Keys are in the storage unit between the seats, as is a GPS. You will set as your destination the restaurant Alouette. It will take you to a safe house in Munich."

I nodded. He made it seem perfectly simple, an "of course" kind of thing. "And you'll take over monitoring the other girls?" I asked.

"Not at this time."

"But something is going on. Something dangerous."

"So far, nothing illegal has happened. They left their country legally and will legally arrive in Germany for a choir tour. We don't have resources to allot to a 'looks fishy' operation just now."

"But . . ."

"Get your charge and bring her in. We'll get you both home safely. Understood?"

"Yes, but . . ."

Reese disappeared, and Colin was back. "He said they're not going to follow the other girls," I said.

"There are several serious matters taking place in Europe right now, and all available agents are assigned. Supervisor Reese is right; nothing illegal has happened with those girls. For all we know, they're going to have a nice musical tour and return home to their parents."

"But . . ." I was sputtering. "You *know* that's not true! They bought Talya a place in this group. She is traveling with false papers. None of the girls' parents are expecting them home!"

"I wish we had the resources to follow up on everything that isn't quite right and make life miserable for all the bad people, Colt, but we just don't. And the fact that Sophie is concerned about this, even inserted her own daughter into whatever is going on, was Sophie's action, not ours. Frankly, we were watching out for her kids as a favor. She doesn't have the authority to open FALCON cases or assign personnel."

"But Talya—"

"Get her out of there."

"What if she won't come?"

"If Talya won't come, it's her decision. She's in Europe now, where she can turn to local authorities for help. We can't allot any further resources—or jeopardize further any resources currently assigned. Meaning you. There's a car waiting for you at the airport. If something goes wrong, there's also one in Munich. Do your best to convince her to leave. And you get out of there."

"But surely FALCON is against human trafficking . . ."

His spoke more quietly. "Of course. And I know how it feels when you're in the midst of something. First, there's no definitive proof we're dealing with something quite so sinister here. Second, we're involved in stopping human trafficking on a very large scale, and that's where agents are thought to be best assigned right now.

"Third, you're new. You've done great, but let's get you out of there before you're in over your head, especially since we don't have teams free to act as backup."

There was a pause. "Do you understand?"

Not only did I understand, I saw the logic. Sophie had a lot of chutzpah to jump into stuff like this without any kind of plan in place and to assume others would clean up her mess. Let alone putting her own daughter at risk.

Or maybe, without backup, I knew I was one lucky sap to have gotten this far, and I had to get out before my inexperience got me or Talya or anybody else killed.

"What happens if she won't come?" I asked.

"You know where the car is parked. We're taking you off the assignment."

And the video feed was gone.

In its place a few minutes later was the information about the car and the instruction to get four hundred euros from an ATM upon landing, to have money in case of emergency.

Flight attendants came around with hot towels, and the captain announced we were approaching Munich. I'd never been to Germany, but all I could think was that I didn't know where the airport parking garage was.

But I had to get Talya. If she was counting on me to follow them, how could I let her know that wasn't an option? How could I let her know she had to come now?

Did I dare text her?

The last thing I wanted was for them to find the

phone on her. Then they'd know she was a plant. They'd have to get rid of her.

Maybe when they were all off the plane, waiting for their luggage, I could text her without anyone noticing. Or maybe she'd text me first.

When we landed, I was one of the first off the plane. I went through immigration before the "girls' choir" even arrived in the line. I followed the others on my flight to the luggage carousel. My own bag, of course, was probably still riding around on a carousel in Dubai. Or maybe someone had marked it as abandoned and blown it up by now.

I got money, as instructed, and asked where the parking garage was located. Then I found a hidden vantage point.

The girls' matching bags arrived before they did. A man from our flight whom I didn't recognize as having been with the girls removed them from the carousel and had them waiting on the floor when the thirteen girls arrived, Talya among them.

Should I text her?

The man and woman who'd traveled with them from Afghanistan were hovering, and the new man was taking charge.

I didn't know what to do. I texted her, "We have to go. I will walk next to you and we will split off."

If she felt the phone vibrate, she made no sign.

It was clear she couldn't read the text without being caught.

Now what?

There was no one at the customs station; they started moving toward one of the exit doors en masse.

I had to take a chance.

I moved out from my hiding place and acted like I was leaving with the rest of the passengers. I fell into step a little ahead of them, so Talya could see me.

She had been forced into the center of the group.

Once we were out of the restricted area, the main terminal opened up into shops and glass and light.

The chaperones were now walking to the sides of their charges, and the other man from the flight was behind them. It took only a second to realize they were all following a thin man in a gray suit. He must have been waiting for them in the terminal. There had been a minimal acknowledgment of him, if any, but they moved crisply along behind him.

How could I make Talya understand she had to get out, now? That no help was coming?

I stopped where I was, turned, and looked straight at her.

As I did, I saw fear in her eyes.

Help me, she mouthed.

Then the group swept past me and she was gone.

CHAPTER SEVENTEEN

Oktoberfest

Outside, the Munich Airport opened up into a plaza, surrounded on three sides by buildings. The ground was red and white, in a pattern of what seemed to be lightning strikes. I'm sure it was supposed to feel airy and cheerful, but to me it felt like a cavern, from which there were few alleys of escape.

My group paid little attention to any of this. They plowed straight ahead.

This is when it occurred to me that the imperative that I "get her out and bring her in" was the agent version of a "million-dollar sentence." Back at school, they offered a lot of interesting seminars and courses, including one on screenwriting. We figured they wanted to give those of us sent to the think tank a way to unleash our agent fantasies. But the seminar leader warned against what Hollywood insiders call "the million-dollar sentence," for example, "the town blows up," or "sixty spaceships descend and unleash dancing pink aliens." Simple remarks that double the budget.

"Get her out and bring her in." So easy to say. So impossible to do.

What were they thinking? I mean, really? We were at an international airport, where there was security out the wazoo. Guards with guns, everywhere. If I grabbed Talya and ran, all the chaperones would have to do is yell and point, and I'd be locked up within minutes. By the time anything got sorted out, the chaperones and girls would all be long gone. And that was assuming I didn't somehow get shot in the melee. It was likely these chaperones had a whole bunch of money invested in the young women who walked in front of me.

At the far end of the enclosed plaza were stairs heading up to street level. There were also stairs descending into the ground.

The girls headed down. I followed, slightly behind.

It was a train station. They were walking with purpose

down the track to the right. Large signs announced you needed your ticket before you boarded the train. And there were large ticket-dispensing machines.

But, again, ticket to where?

The girls stood together, well down the platform, and faced the empty track farthest to the right. I read the signs over their heads. Apparently three different trains ran on that track. Which one would the girls be taking?

Lights approached from down the track. Was that their train? Which ticket should I buy? What should I do? I had only minutes, at most.

I fished out the credit card, aware of the line building behind me. And I bought three tickets, one for each destination on track three.

The arriving train's information was color-coded in red above the doors. It ran to and from Munich, which was, according to the posted map, about twenty miles away. Colin had said there was another "safe" car in Munich. I might have to go for that one.

Silver doors slid open, and the passengers piled out, heading quickly toward the escalators and the airport terminal.

By the time the platform cleared, there was no sign of the girls. They must have embarked. The doors were closing as I jumped aboard.

Domino twelve.

The train was not full. I could see down through open connecting doors that they were in one of the first cars. I took a moment to mourn the safety represented by the airport car we'd never drive. Not to mention that Ms. Bossy-Pants could have seen how well I drove, after all.

One good thing was that thirteen girls in tunics and headscarves were easy to keep an eye on, even several train cars ahead. I settled into a seat, with an empty seat next to me and two vacant seats across. And I pondered what to do.

According to the map, there were seven stops between the airport and the major metropolis that was Munich. If they got off before Munich, I would too. But I bet they were riding all the way in. Which gave me approximately forty-five minutes to hatch a plan.

The train stopped at a station. I looked out the window and was surprised at how rural the landscape was. A few folks filtered on, but the choirgirls didn't move. The next stop was in a larger town. More folks embarked. The noise level in the car rose noticeably. By the third town, the train was filling up. A guy and a girl came and asked, in German (with accompanying hand signals), if the seats across from me were taken. I shook my head. Obviously not.

They sat. It took a moment before I looked at them, but when I did, I was startled. They were smiling and in a really good mood. The young man, who seemed not much older than I, had tousled blond hair and ruddy cheeks. His jaw was chiseled, and his cheeks were naturally rounded and a bit flushed. He wore a white linen shirt, with rounded buttons. And lederhosen. Seriously. Lederhosen. Brown leather shorts with attached suspenders. Knee socks. And funny brown boot-shoes. I thought this getup only existed in movies and commercials for beer. What could possibly possess a seemingly normal young man to put on such a thing?

And then I looked at the girl sitting next to him. She was costumed also, in a white blouse, green vest with a tightly cinched waist, and an embroidered apron over a skirt. But that wasn't really the first thing I noticed. The first thing I noticed was that the square neckline of her dress was cut down to . . . well, pretty low. And there were ruffles that matched the apron, happily adorning the square.

Her hair was loose and curled, her lips sapphire red. She had black ribbons in her hair.

I looked up. To my astonishment, they were not the only passengers dressed like refugees from a cuckoo clock. The whole freaking train car was filled with old men, young men, middle-aged men . . . in shorts and embroidered suspenders. They wore silly hats and carried instruments. One had a tuba. The women of all ages wore laced bodices that gave them a fitted waist, ballooning skirts in a variety of colors and patterns, covered by an apron, and square necklines that formed a frame designed to show things off to advantage.

The boy spoke again, in a friendly tone.

I smiled in response. "I'm sorry, I don't speak German," I said.

"It's all right, I speak some English," he said. "I'm Hans. This is Addie." The girl heard her name and smiled.

"Where are you going?" I asked and motioned to the filling train car.

"Munich," he said, with a grin. "Oktoberfest! Aren't you coming?"

"But it's September," I said.

He shrugged good-naturedly. "It ends in early October."

"Why is everyone dressed like this?" I asked. "What's at Oktoberfest?"

He leaned forward. "Beer," he said. "And girls! Lots of both. You should come!"

This was adding to my international education, but I needed to get back to the task at hand. "I'd love to," I said. "But I don't have any lederhosen."

"No problem," said Hans, "I've got an extra set."

You'd know it. "That's nice, but I have to meet a friend," I said.

"Bring him along."

"It's a girl."

"Even better."

Hans said something to Addie that caused to her respond affirmatively.

"She has a spare dirndl," said Hans.

"A what?"

"The dress. With the apron and everything. We're wearing our good ones—the ones handed down through the family. But we're staying in Munich tonight. We brought fresh new ones for tomorrow, in case these get stained. But who cares if they do, really?"

In spite of everything, I had a quick flash of what Talya would look like wearing a dirndl. Too bad we weren't heading for the safe house, with time for a night on the town.

But then . . .

"Really? You have lederhosen that might fit me?"

"We seem about the same size," said Hans.

"And a dirndl?"

Addie heard the question and nodded yes.

After a quick exchange, I had the lederhosen and the dirndl, with all their various components, in my carry-on. The restroom, which was in our car, was seldom occupied; it was a pretty short trip for everyone.

I took out my phone and typed in, "RESTROOM. NOW." Then I held my breath.

Somehow, Talya was able to glance at her phone. My guess was, she was scared enough to start taking risks.

Through all the standing passengers, I saw her jump to her feet with her hand over her mouth, as if she was about to be sick. With a crazed look in her eye, she bolted past her handlers and up into the next car, heading for mine.

I stood and rushed into the vacant toilet, leaving the door unlocked, praying no one else would feel the call of nature before Talya could get here.

The seconds ticked by before the silver door handle bounced downward and the door panel opened inward. I flattened myself against the back wall, to make room.

It was her! Thank God.

She came in and fell back against the door, shutting it.

"Colt," she said, her voice trembling. "They're drugging us! And they're coming! What do we do?"

I'd never seen Talya so frightened and seemingly helpless.

"Take a breath," I said. "We have to work fast." I unzipped my bag. "We change."

"Here? Now?"

"There's no other choice. I'll turn around."

I had gotten her all the pieces of the folk outfit, and I dug out my own. The restroom was small, and even with the bag resting on the toilet itself, there was barely floor space for both of us. I swapped out my shirt first, then took off my jeans and pulled on the shorts. They were heavier than I expected and made of brown leather. The knee socks were scratchy, but on they came.

I turned back. Talya's tunic was on the floor. I stuffed it and her headscarf into the bag. She was trying to button the blouse, but her fingers were trembling. I took over; she let me finish. She held on to my shoulder for balance as she stepped into the skirt and added stockings.

"Is this going to work?" she whispered.

"It has to," I said. And I laced up her vest. "Do you have a hairbrush?" When she shook her head, I handed her a comb.

Even over the mechanical sounds of the train, we heard footfalls approaching, and a banging on the door.

"I'll go first. I'm across the aisle and down a few rows. When this person moves on, come over and sit by me."

Another banging, and terse words in Pashto.

I took a breath, opened the door enough to slide out, and said in an animated voice, "Hold your horses! I'm coming out!"

I looked down on one of the men I recognized from the airport and tried to act nonchalant and happily on my way to get soused.

He looked at me, shocked. I clearly wasn't whom he expected. He looked forward, into to the next car, then back at me. Anger clouded his face. He started making his way forward through the crowds.

I swung my bag out of the restroom and quickly headed back to take the aisle seat across from Addie and Hans, both of whom found my transformation highly enjoyable.

The bathroom door slid open, and I turned enough to catch Talya's eye. She flew down the crowded aisle and I moved my legs out of the way, motioning her to slide to the inside seat against the window, which she did.

"This is my cousin . . . Susan," I said by way of introduction.

"Very happy to meet you," said Hans, and from the glint in his eye, it seemed the truth.

Addie, however, was studying her with a critical eye. After a moment, she took a small bag out of her satchel and removed some makeup. She held up a tube of bright red lipstick, and Talya nodded yes. Delighted, Addie got to work. I hoped she couldn't tell how petrified both of her seatmates were, but we both did our best to join in the merriment. Eyeliner, mascara, and blush were next, and when Addie finished with her hairbrush and sat back to present her handiwork, I had to gasp.

The girl seated next to me was the farthest thing from a scarved Afghan girl you could imagine. She was a vivacious, luscious Bavarian, headed for a good time.

But would it work to hide her in plain sight?

Because it was very apparent that the handlers of the Afghan girls were in a state of high alert. The man who had come first, banging on the bathroom door, had obviously made it to the back of the train and, not finding his missing choirgirl, had notified the others. The two other men were now going seat by seat and performing a thorough search of each toilet. One man was shorter, with close-cropped hair and the coloring of a someone of Middle Eastern origin. The other was tall and skinny, with a milky-white complexion and dark gray hair. Neither of them looked at all pleasant.

The shorter man passed our seats first. As he arrived, Talya and I became animated, laughing heartily and making like we were happy Oktoberfesters. He passed without a pause.

As he did, the train slowed to a stop at the next stop; no one got off, but loads more passengers crowded in. I saw both men step off the train and watch the platform for any fleeing girls. They found none.

As the train lurched off again, I looked at the map above. We were only one stop from Munich now. Passengers pressed in on us, and a couple of people scooted their bags on the floor by us and stood, holding on to the back of the seats. This effectively made a screen between us and the two men, who were having a much harder time of moving through the aisles.

As they met up in the middle of the train, I could see from the corner of my eye that they were perplexed. And furious.

I leaned forward and took another look at Talya. She had risen to the occasion and was chatting merrily with Hans. For the first time, I had a new worry. For while she looked nothing like an Afghan choirgirl, she looked exactly like Talya Ellis, dressed up for a theme album cover.

We pulled out of the station and began zipping toward the cityscape of Munich.

Dear God, if you get us out of this alive, I started . . . what? What could I promise? I didn't even know what my bargaining chips were. I couldn't promise to stay home, as I was on a new track. I couldn't promise to obey my mother, because what if she didn't want me to go, but I thought I was supposed to, that God wanted me to?

If you get us out of this alive, I will be very, very grateful.

I studied Talya, with her brushed hair bouncing, her cheeks glowing, her breasts crowded together, framed by the white ruffles. How could every guy in the world not be tempted to look at her? And how could *none* of them recognize her?

And that's an understatement, dear God, I added.

CHAPTER EIGHTEEN

Munich

As the train arrived at the Hauptbahnhof, Munich's main train station, passengers began to jockey for positions to disembark. In all the noise and excitement, I had neglected to look at my watch. I did now. The small message light was lit. I pressed the button, and a screen came up. It was a map with the Hauptbahnhof in one corner and, several blocks away, a throbbing blue dot. I assumed this was our car. Could it be we were this close to safety?

Talya and I said good-bye to Hans and Addie. I had the name of the beer garden they were going to visit on a piece of paper, along with their home address so I could return our outfits if we didn't catch up. Hans had said it was okay; it would be a crime to take my cousin out of the dress.

The sooner the better, was my thought in reply.

The station itself was sprawling, with many tracks coming in and heading out. We'd come in on a track that was below ground. The Afghani girls were standing. Their handlers waited until most of the others had left the car to herd them out. They were not taking any chances. The group was huddled together, the chaperones keeping them close in. The men looked back several times, but it was clear they thought the girl was lost. How? Had she jumped from the train? If so, they certainly weren't contacting the local authorities.

Since the choirgirls were heading to the escalator at the front of the train, I grabbed Talya's arm and turned toward the one at the rear of the platform.

Much to my surprise, she shook her head. "I've got to see," she said.

So we turned around and followed the girls up and through the glass-and-concrete terminal, hanging back at a safe distance.

My blood pressure was sky high. Not because I was sure they'd see us—there were likely a hundred people between us and them—but because all the signs overhead were in a language I couldn't understand. We were somewhere I'd never been—a foreign country—and, for the first time, I didn't have any adult showing me around or telling me what to do.

I knew where the car was, but that was it.

Did Germans drive on the right or left side of the street? All I wanted to do was get Talya to the safe house and collapse. Perhaps that much I could handle.

Outside, the air was bracing, and the sky was full of gray clouds. It didn't look like it was going to rain, but you couldn't tell for sure. The threat of precipitation didn't seem to be dampening anybody's mood.

Talya and I hung back by the terminal doors and watched the girls being led to a small autobus. It was silver—even the windows were tinted silver, so you couldn't see inside—and looked to hold only about twenty people. Which was about what they had, counting the chaperones. There were no banners that said "The Very Best Afghani Girls' Choir Tour" or anything like that. In fact, it was as nondescript as possible. Talya surreptitiously snapped a photo of the license plate.

And then, just as the last couple of girls were about to be herded up the steps, the tall white man grabbed the last one by the arm, whispered something to her, and led her around the front of the bus.

We couldn't see where they went from there.

I looked at my watch, trying to get a lock on my directions concerning the station and the car, when Talya stood stock-still.

"That was AnaSophia," she said. "They've taken AnaSophia!"

The girl had been wearing a muted orange-colored tunic and a cream-colored scarf. I hadn't gotten a very good look at her face, but from a distance, she seemed very pretty. The fear had been apparent in her brown eyes.

"I'm sorry," I said. "I've got to get you out of here."

I placed myself in the real-world position that echoed the blue blinking dot on the watch screen. Then I grabbed Talya's arm and began to steer her away from the station. She came with me, still looking over her shoulder. We couldn't tell where AnaSophia had been taken.

It wasn't our job, anyway.

As we walked the street, it occurred to me that Talya still seemed under the influence of some kind of medication. She wasn't as sharp as usual, and she kept banging into me as she tried to walk straight.

Several blocks down and over, on a much quieter side street, we stood beside a black BMW, which made sense, as we were in Germany. It was an M3 coupe, and it had a blue light flashing inside. I'd seen that in the United States when people had activated their security systems, but this one matched the blue dot on my watch. In fact, as I glanced at my watch again, I noticed that there was a faint blue glow radiating from underneath one of the side buttons.

I pushed it. The driver's-side door popped open.

I unlocked the passenger's side, walked Talya around, shoved her in, and shut the door before getting in on the driver's side. I locked the doors.

There was no window-mounted GPS. I picked up the key that was in the center console and turned on the car. Then I saw a little round button by the gearshift that seemed to control the front panel. It also had a button that said "nav." Of course. I hit it and the navigation screen bounced to life. I hit buttons on the screen until I found the one that gave me restaurants, and there it was, that wonderful French option about which Colin had spoken: Alouette. I hit the button and watched in relief as a map came to life before me.

The safe house wasn't far. Three or four miles, tops.

As I studied the gear stick, feeling my way around

how the car drove, Talya's hand fell heavily onto my arm. I looked at her.

She was crying.

"What?" I said. I knew she'd been drugged, but I'd never seen her in any sort of position of weakness, and this really threw me off.

"They've taken AnaSophia," she said.

"I know. I'm sorry." This didn't seem to help. "Look, I am sorry. But there's nothing we can do."

In response, she held up the phone I'd given her. On the front display was a map, with a small red dot on it. The dot was moving.

"You were able to put the tracking disk on her," I said.

Talya nodded.

I folded my arms across the black leather steering wheel and rested my head there, trying to find the words to explain things to her.

"Talya, I'm sorry. We're off the mission. Actually, you know what? There was no mission. Your mom sent you into this thing entirely on her own. I had one objective: to keep anyone from kidnapping or injuring you or Thorne on your tour. That's *it*. FALCON never allocated resources to you running off into some international girls-not-really-singing scheme. They don't have the resources to direct that way now, even if they wanted to. We're off the case. That's it."

I looked over to see if she got it.

Tears were now pouring down her cheeks.

I said, "We can't go after her. I don't know my way around Germany. At all. We have no backup."

She said nothing.

"I can't go driving off, trying to follow a dot on a phone. I don't know the roads. I've been told to bring you in to a safe house. Anything else, I've gone rogue. I want to be an agent. I don't want to get fired on my first frickin' assignment."

"This was your first assignment?" she asked.

I groaned. "First and quite possibly the last."

She was staring at the navigation screen, which I took to be a good thing. Then she opened the console between us and rummaged around. She found a cable with a silver insertion tip at each end. She plugged one into the jack on the side of the car's GPS. She plugged the other into my phone. And, in a moment, the red dot from the phone screen popped up, blinking, onto the GPS screen. "Go half a block and turn left," said the friendly female voice.

Oh, crap. Seriously.

"I don't care if you're on a mission or not," she said.

"If we don't go after AnaSophia, no one else will. She will be gone. And every minute of every day, you will have to live with the fact that she's out there, somewhere, kidnapped, and it's your fault."

What was Thorne and Talya's dad like? I mean, if their mom—and Talya—were like this? How many times had Mrs. Ellis said, "Can you mow the lawn today, honey? Oh, yeah, and save the world? 'Cause if you don't, it'll be your fault Thailand blows up?"

Talya looked down then. "Our fault," she corrected quietly. "It will be *our* fault."

"Talya. It would be stupid. We'd be walking into a dangerous situation with no weapons and no backup. At least now I have you, out and safe. What if, instead of gaining her, both of us get killed?"

I am not Dix. I am not the hero. I am the also-ran.

"What if we don't?"

"It's dangerous."

"We could try."

The prudent thing would be to drive Talya and myself to the safe house. Within a day, we could be home in New Jersey, drinking Arnold Palmers with Thorne and telling wild stories about Afghanistan. More than anything, that's what I wanted to do.

Only now, getting this crazy girl home safely

wouldn't feel like a win. It wouldn't be like we'd gone through something bizarre together and survived. Every time I thought of her, it would be with regret.

More than that, I remembered my class in ethics. The way to make the best ethical decision always comes down to: You don't do what's easy. You do what's right.

I looked at the flashing dot. The map on the screen was pulling back farther as the dot traveled away from us. AnaSophia. The girl Talya had risked her own life to save.

"Okay. Okay," I said. We could try.

Domino thirteen.

"If the situation is too dangerous, if there's no chance we can pull her out, we bail. Understood?"

Talya nodded. I turned on the car.

Fortunately, in Germany, cars drive on the right-hand side, like they do at home. I silently thanked the person who had programmed the coupe's navigation system to speak in English and pulled out into traffic.

We made a couple of turns and ended up on a wide boulevard called Prinzregentenplatz (which, even with my limited German, I took to be Prince Regent Street). We crossed a river and found our way onto Highway A8.

The dot was only a few miles ahead of us, and they

turned onto what seemed to be another giant highway, this one called A1. We headed in that direction.

I said, "Tell me what's going on. How do you know the girls aren't just on a choir tour?"

"They drugged us," she said.

"But that might have been just to keep everybody calm and not causing trouble," I said. "You know, like some people give their dogs tranquilizers before they get on a plane."

"Girls are not dogs," she said, still sounding groggy. "And the girls told me, before I got there, that they took photographs of each of them just in their underwear. That doesn't happen if you are going to get a job at a sewing factory."

Okay. She had me there.

We'd been in the car like half an hour or forty minutes when we ended up on the A1. When I looked over at Talya, she was asleep. Not asleep as much as passed out.

It was then that a crisp male voice said, "Colt. What are you doing?"

CHAPTER NINETEEN

Going Rogue

"SIR?" I SAID.

It didn't sound like Colin.

"This is Supervisor Reese. We had you tagged in the car by the station. You programmed in the route to the safe house. You should have been there by now. Instead, you're heading east on the A1. What are you doing?"

"Talya was able to put the tracking disk on AnaSophia, one of the girls from Afghanistan, who is a family friend. For some reason, they split her off from the other girls, and are taking her somewhere. You said there was no one to intervene with the girls. So . . . so we're following her."

"'We're'? You have Talya Ellis?"

"Yes, sir."

"You have Talya Ellis. Then your assignment is officially over. Turn around now and head back to the safe house."

I glanced at Talya. She was still out cold. I took a deep breath. "We have reason to believe that AnaSophia has been kidnapped," I said.

"I told you, we have no resources to bring this to resolution." His voice was tight.

Dear God, was I really doing this?

"I'm a resource," I said. "And my last assignment is over."

"Colt, you're not trained." Supervisor Reese was clearly exasperated.

"We're just going to try to grab her. If things get out of hand, we'll get out of there."

Like "grabbing" Talya had been a piece of cake. There was a pause. "Is Colin around?" I asked, hopefully.

"No. You were supposed to be resolved by now. We couldn't spare him in the field any longer, so he's off on assignment."

Of course he was. They couldn't keep a top agent around as a tether for a teenager forever.

There was a pause. I knew Reese was trying to frame the consequences of me not following orders. Once he outlined those consequences, I would have no other choices than to obey or be in whatever deep trouble he outlined.

"Sir, I'll return the car and Talya as soon as possible," I said.

And I turned off the speaker.

In that whole conversation, the worst news was that Colin was gone. I had come to rely on the fact that he was there and in my corner. I desperately needed his advice right that very minute. I tried hard to remember what he'd told me when things had taken an unexpected turn back in Afghanistan. I fact, I'd jotted it down and had mulled it over since.

The assignment you're given is seldom the assignment you end up on. But when there's a course of action before you, you first decide if it's the best course, given the circumstances. Then you fully commit. On assignments, there is no time for dithering. You review, you decide, you act. You don't keep looking back, two forks in the road ago, thinking, "What the hell happened?" Only, "What's the best course of action, given the current circumstances?"

What was the best course of action, given the current circumstances?

I hunkered down and followed the dot.

After half an hour, I began to get nervous. Why had Supervisor Reese not returned? It seemed a major operation was going down, and he obviously had more to worry about than some newbie off driving through the countryside. Or maybe he was trying to find someone to follow us. More likely he was just following my little blue dot out of the corner of his eye while focusing on the team that was trying to save the world from nuclear annihilation.

After another few minutes, we came to a traffic circle and went partway around to join another road. Now what? I reached over and jostled Talya. She snuffled. I jostled her again, hard.

She sat bolt upright, her eyes wide, staring around. "What?" she said. "What?"

Then she looked over and saw me. I watched the pieces of the puzzle slowly find their places in her mind.

"Where are we?" she asked.

"Beats me," I answered. "Somewhere in the Austrian Alps."

She looked at the navigation unit and saw the flashing light. "You're still following her?"

"Yes."

"How long?"

"Since we left the train station? Over an hour."

"No idea where we're going?"

"Could you study the sat nav? It would be helpful."

She wiped sleep from her eyes. "Got anything to eat or drink?"

"Help yourself to anything in the carry-on."

She grabbed it from the backseat. I had stuffed bottled water and half a sandwich in there from the plane along with the entire "Welcome to First Class" package. She drank the whole bottle. "We seem to be heading for Berchtesgaden," she said. "It's a really pretty town in the Bavarian Alps."

As she said that, we were prompted to make a really hard left onto Berchtesgadener Strasse, a very slim mountain road alongside a railroad track. I began to concentrate on gaining back some of the distance between ourselves and AnaSophia's car.

"Have they stopped?" she asked. "For gas or anything?"

"No," I said. "No one's gotten in or out of the car. How are you feeling?"

"More clearheaded," she said. "Much more clearheaded."

She munched. We drove. But as we came through the mountain pass and approached the town of Berchtesgaden, GPS lady instructed us to head off to the right. Then to the left. Then another right. Then a hairpin left.

We passed some buildings and a long parking lot with some tour buses in it. But the car in front of us hadn't stopped. It was plowing up ahead.

"Holy cow," Talya said. "They're going to the Kehlsteinhaus."

"Where?"

"The Kehlsteinhaus. Eagle's Nest. The chalet on a ridge of the Kehlstein mountain that was built for Hitler."

"What? Are you sure?"

"That's the only place this road goes. And you're not supposed to drive there. It's closed to the public. You have to take a bus."

Even as she spoke, we approached a local policeman in the middle of the road. He wore a smart black uniform, and motioned for us to stop. I did. I put down the window.

He said something stern in German.

Talya leaned over me and said something back, also in German.

He asked another question; she answered. Then he asked something else, his eyebrow raised. She looked at her outfit, and mine, and laughed. *"Un Feier,"* she said, shook her head and laughed. *"Nein Bier,"* she said. *"Nein."* She held up her water bottle and the remains of the sandwich.

"All right," said the policeman, now in English, "but drive very carefully."

I nodded seriously and headed up the winding road.

"You speak German?" I asked.

"No," she answered. "Well, I speak broken German. He could tell immediately I was an American. My Pashto is much better."

"So, what's going on?"

"I said our uncle just went up. He told us to come; it was an emergency. The cop said, 'So it is your cousin who is ill?' I said it was. He asked why we were dressed like this—"

"And you said we'd been at a party. With no beer."

"It is that time of year."

I drove ahead carefully but quickly, in case the officer changed his mind.

The road was beautiful. One side ran along the side of a mountain, while the other had a guardrail framing endless views of Alps. Wow.

"Have you been here before?" I asked, trying to keep my mind off what was ahead. According to the GPS, the vehicle we'd been following had preceded us up the mountain road, past a daunting hairpin turn, and had come to a stop. The good thing was, this road seemed to only go one place and there were no other exits.

The bad news was, an inevitable confrontation was waiting for us.

"Once Thorne and I wrote the songs for an album while staying in Garmisch two summers ago. We took day trips around Bavaria and Salzburg. Where we're going is called Kehlsteinhaus, which is German for, well, house on the Kehlstein. Which is this mountain. In English, it's usually called Eagle's Nest."

"You said something about Hitler?" As we drove, we passed through tunnels that had been blasted through the mountain. So far, I'd counted three.

"Yeah. Bormann had this made as a present from the Nazis to Hitler for his fiftieth birthday. Joke was, after spending what would be millions of dollars today, Hitler never liked it. He didn't feel safe stuck up so high. And he didn't like the elevator."

"Why not?"

"Maybe it's because twelve men died just blasting out the elevator path and installing it. Or maybe being in the middle of a mountain made him feel claustrophobic. Whatever. The fact that Hitler barely ever came and stayed less than half an hour when he did is what made the local government able to persuade the Allies to leave it intact. It's now a popular tourist site."

"You are a walking encyclopedia," I said.

"I generally only remember the juicy stuff," she said.

"Like what else?"

"Martin Bormann, who built it, and even Eva Braun, used the Kehlsteinhouse much more."

"Eva Braun? She was Hitler's wife?"

"Well, he only married her hours before they committed suicide. Hitler never showed off Eva; partly because he thought he had to be perceived as a knight-errant, who, by definition, is single. Partly because he didn't think Eva was a great asset. So she never got to go to any big Reich parties or anything. *Until*... until Eva's sister, Gretl, married Hermann Fegelein, a prominent Nazi, up here at Eagle's Nest. After that, Eva got to go to the parties as Fegelein's sister-in-law."

"They had the wedding here?"

"Yup."

We came to a final, long tunnel that ran into the darkness of the mountain.

I took a deep breath.

"We're really doing this," I said.

The headlights came on as I drove on through.

CHAPTER TWENTY

Going Up

ONCE WE'D GONE through the tunnel and taken a final curve, we found the parking lot was nearly empty. They were closing up for the day. One final orange and white tour bus was there, the door already closed, and a guide with a clipboard taking attendance to make certain everyone was back on board to leave.

Rising before us was a mountain; in its center was a fancy mouse-hole-shaped tunnel entrance, with an imposing stone wall surrounding it. To the left was a small stone house. To the right was a ticket window, and a covered plaza where ticket holders could wait their turn.

If you looked straight up, four hundred feet—forty stories—directly above the tunnel entrance, on the ledge of the mountain, sat a stone chalet.

I parked over to the far side, where the only other vehicles remained. There were a couple of other cars, presumably belonging to the people who worked here. We had no idea which vehicle belonged to our quarry.

"Any ideas?" I asked.

"We need to get up there. There is a footpath, but it takes a long time. They could have traded her off to someone else and gone up and down in the elevator by the time we climbed it."

"So, we get to take this famous elevator," I said.

"Here's something that not everyone knows," Talya said. "The elevator is unusual. It's two stories."

"What?"

"There's an upper car that the guests ride in, and below it is another car that stops at the floor below to bring up supplies for the kitchens."

"You mean they're attached?"

"Yep. There's only one shaft. So there's an entrance to the service elevator a floor below where tourists get on, and once you get to the top, the kitchen floor is right below where you get off into the Kehlsteinhaus itself."

"How does this help us?"

"It might be easier to sneak up on the service elevator if everything is closing. Come on. We've got to go."

We got out of the car and walked across the nearly vacant lot toward the side door that Talya said would take us to the lower car of the elevator. The ticket man shut his window and I jumped. As we headed for the smaller entrance, two men came walking out of it together.

Before they could see us, in the space of seconds, Talya grabbed my arm and pulled me out of the line of sight—and into the tunnel leading to the main elevator. No one was there taking tickets. It was clearly closed for the night.

"Run!" Talya said.

The tunnel was very long. And straight. Nowhere to hide.

Without stopping to question, I ran.

The tunnel went on and on. And on. A series of light fixtures dotted the center of the curved ceiling. What was Talya doing? If anyone looked in here and saw us running, the jig would be up. But she was going full tilt, and making very fast progress.

Within a couple of minutes, she had gotten to the end of the tunnel and disappeared.

I was steps behind.

The tunnel emptied into a large circular room. My first and only thought was to get out of the sightline of the tunnel, which I did, by joining Talya against the red stone wall to the right. From there, I looked at the focal point of the room.

The elevator. It was flanked by electrified wall candelabras on either side of the closed doors. Somehow this added to the feeling that we'd stumbled into the lair of some evil genius from many, many years ago.

As I tried to catch my breath, a man's voice echoed down the tunnel behind us, calling out something in German. Talya looked at me and shook her head.

They apparently didn't know we were down here. He was calling to make certain all his coworkers were gone.

He hit a switch, and all the lights went off. We were plunged into total darkness.

Then came the sound of the large metal doors that guarded the entrance being dragged shut. They closed with finality.

"We're locked in," I said.

"The elevator," she whispered.

Together, we felt our way along the wall toward the elevator. Talya crashed into something and muttered under her breath. It was a trash can. I skirted around it, and as I reached the wall on the other side of it, I felt a round button.

I pushed it. The doors slid open.

It revealed the remains of a bygone era.

The top half of the car was polished brass, illuminated by a circular chandelier with eight round light bulbs. Directly in front of us was a round mirror. Thank God the electrics were still on, although who knew how long they would be?

We walked in.

Domino fourteen.

Talya slammed her open palm on the "up" button, and the door slid shut.

To the right of the doors was a large brass clock, which said it was now 5:11. Below it was a black telephone from the 1930s, complete with rotary dial. It was like we'd stepped back into history. Bormann and Hitler and Eva Braun could have used this very telephone.

There was a whirr of machinery. The car began the ascent.

I looked at Talya. She looked up, seemingly eager.

The elevator continued its ascent. I was praying for wisdom about what to do when we got there when something happened that sent a shudder straight through me.

The telephone rang.

Talya and I froze. Somehow, I felt like we'd entered the Twilight Zone, and if I picked it up, Herr Hitler would be on the other end. Although, of course, he didn't like this elevator. Or the shaft that twelve men had died blasting out.

Talya's eyes were huge. She shook her head, although she didn't need to. There was no one on the other end of that phone to whom we had anything to say.

We didn't answer.

It stopped ringing.

We expelled the breath I hadn't realized we'd both been holding.

Then the lights went out.

The elevator stopped.

We were stuck in the middle of the mountain.

Apparently, they'd called to make certain no one was in here. Then they'd shut down for the night.

Now what? Would we be stuck here till morning?

Talya only hesitated a second.

"We need a light," she said. "What have you got on your phone or your watch?"

My phone had a flashlight app. I turned it on. "Up," she said. "Up."

I shone it toward the top of the car. The ceiling was done in grand style also, with wood and brass. And in the center was the removable panel to get to the top of the elevator for work.

"Give me a boost," she said.

"What?"

She grabbed onto my shoulders; I cupped my hands to give her a boost, and next thing I knew, she was on my shoulders, pushing the panel opening aside.

"You coming?" she asked. And she hoisted herself onto the top of the elevator.

How? There was no one to give me a boost.

I could boost up from the top of the mats they'd put around the bottom half of the car to keep tourists from wrecking the paneling. But there was nothing to grab hold of to climb to the top of the car. I wasn't going to be the one to wreck the historic mirror. Not going to happen.

Then I checked the brass clock. It seemed secured to the wall pretty tightly.

I gave it a try. One foot on the mat, one on the clock, I was able to climb close enough to grab the brass along the top. From there, I could get a hold of the opening in the top of the car. I pushed off from the clock—and fell back down onto the floor of the car.

"Come *on*," said Talya.

I went through the whole process again. This time, she grabbed my shoulders and pulled me, hard, till I was panting next to her on the top of the elevator car.

The shaft was cold. And quiet.

And very, very dark.

"Light," she said. I knelt and hit my flashlight app again.

The shaft was small, the size of the car. The four walls were flax colored, smooth, maybe made of concrete or flat stone. The side on which the elevator doors opened was smooth and empty. There were steel girders along two of the other walls. And on the fourth wall, the wall against which the steel cable holding the elevator went up, was a ladder. A ladder with very wide rungs, which protruded about a foot and a half from the wall. The cable ran up and down alongside the middle of it. The ladder continued up, off into the darkness of space.

Lucky us.

"Let's get going," said Talya.

There seemed no other choice. How many stories were still above us? If we were about in the middle of the shaft, it would be about the size of twenty floors above, twenty floors below.

Who hasn't wanted to climb a twenty-story ladder in the dark? What could possibly go wrong?

I looked at her and at the dirndl with the skirt and sighed. "I'll go first."

Not waiting for a reply, I hoisted myself up onto the first rung.

It was a weird ladder. The rungs, if they really were that, were like two feet apart. It was tricky to figure out where to hold on to boost yourself up. It was also strange to have that huge cable right in the center of the ladder, going up. I wasn't sure what would happen if the elevator started. If you weren't prepared, the cable suddenly moving might slice you in half.

But it was shut down for the night. Right?

I knew in situations like this, the trick was always to look up, not down.

Up, not down.

Feet on rung, hoist yourself up, grab side bar above, hoist yourself up.

Once, my foot slipped off the rung, and I grabbed

tight, adrenaline surging. But there was no time to stop. I couldn't if I wanted to. Talya was behind me, climbing like a monkey.

And she was in a hurry.

"Go!" she said. "AnaSophia needs us!"

It was after we'd been climbing for a good ten minutes, maybe making it up eight or ten floors' worth of height, that we heard a strange sound. A whirring. And suddenly, the shaft was flooded with light.

Someone had turned the electrics back on. And that could only mean one thing.

"Climb over to the side!" I hollered. "Get away from the center cable!"

No sooner had we both flung ourselves away from the center of the ladder than the cable started to move. And the elevator began to disappear below us.

Round lights ran up one corner of the shaft, about ten feet apart. One per story. There were maybe a dozen above us.

And, as the elevator sunk toward the earth, there were many, many below.

What now?

There were endless possibilities of what might happen next, but we had no way of guessing which it would be. There seemed no point in going down. There seemed no point in staying where we were. The only other choice was up. Fast.

Who hasn't wanted to climb a forty-story ladder? With no safety net?

The elevator itself was now a small dark square, far below. It came to a stop, presumably at the base.

We both continued hoisting ourselves up from rung to rung, with as much speed as possible. Even though the elevator was stationary, both of us stayed on the small piece of rung away from the center cable.

I was half expecting the lights to be shut off again at any moment.

We'd only made it up another four rungs or so when there was another humming noise. The steel in the middle began to vibrate.

The elevator began to rise.

Crap. If someone was on the elevator, they must have noticed the open panel in the ceiling. And why would it be coming up if no one was on it?

My main concern was that neither of us get crushed. Which was always a worthy goal.

"Talya, when it comes, let yourself fall on top of it, but as quietly as possible. And lie flat," I said. I couldn't tell how much extra space would be between the elevator car and the shaft's ceiling.

We looked down. The elevator was approaching quickly.

I didn't want to think about what would happen if one of us made a wrong move.

The car was coming at a regulated pace. That made it easier to anticipate its arrival. It reached Talya first. She let go of the ladder, let her weight sink onto the car, and lay down. I immediately did the same, and ended up on top of her for a brief moment. I rolled off. Soundlessly, she dragged herself over to the open panel and peeked through.

"Nobody," she said.

She swung her legs down, grabbed onto the side of the opening, and lowered herself through, making the final drop as quietly as possible. I did the same. If there was anyone riding up, he was in the service car below. Was it possible he didn't hear the thuds as we dropped in?

We didn't have time to discuss it, because no sooner had I hit the floor and stood straight than the car came to a stop and the doors slid open in front of us.

CHAPTER TWENTY-ONE

On the Ledge

THE ROPES THAT held the tourists back were slack and to the side. The reception hall around us was empty; however, down the hall, straight in front of us, stood a large man in a suit. His skin wasn't as white as most of the Germans', more of a gingerbread, but I couldn't take a guess at his nationality.

Talya stepped out, smoothing her skirt as though she was a flustered teen. "I forgot my purse!" she said, in English with a German accent.

The man stared at her like she was crazy, but he didn't move.

I followed as she flounced to the right, toward the open door to what proved to be a wood-paneled dining room, the ceiling wood as well. Scores of empty tables with red cloths lined the room. A long wooden bar, now unmanned, ran along one wall.

The entire room was empty.

"Where are they?" she whispered.

We were quiet, and listened.

Nothing.

She nodded forward, and we both crept toward glass doors to a terrace. It was long and thin and ran the length of the building. It was lined by a series of very large arched windows, each of which framed a picture-perfect view of the mountains; mountain peaks rose from a floor of clouds below us. Which meant we were awfully high up.

We heard footsteps, and a thin man, tall and wan, with a long, pointed nose and small, dark eyes, paced past. He wore a white shirt and black pants and he smoked a cigarette. In one hand he carried a small black book. He kept balancing the book and the cigarette in one hand to check his watch. He was nervous.

He resumed pacing.

"He's wearing a name tag," I whispered. We both ducked again as he walked by.

"I think he works here," Talya answered. "Maybe he's so nervous because he's let people up, but no one's supposed to still be here."

He turned and walked back into the Kehlsteinhaus through a door at the far end of the terrace to our right.

"He's waiting for someone. But where are they?"

Talya made a bold decision, beckoning me to follow her as she scooted out the doors onto the newly vacated terrace and turned in the opposite direction, hurrying quickly to the door to outside. Together, we ran up the six stone stairs that led outside.

The view outside was startlingly beautiful. The view of the Alps, with their lakes of clouds dipping below, went on for miles. I looked up the mountain and was shocked to find that, even twenty feet away, I couldn't see a thing. It seemed these clouds settled where they pleased.

From this vantage point, you could see that the Kehlsteinhaus was a large rectangular stone chalet with a roof that sloped down on both sides from a ridge in the center. A large, half-oval flagstone open-air terrace protruded from the back, populated by empty seats and a small wooden hut toward the rear. A large stone walkway continued up the mountain, but at the moment, it was hard to tell just how far up it went.

At the same time, we heard voices muttering above us, inside the gray condensation. Talya moved forward, stopping behind the brown hut. I knelt beside her, and we listened.

"So, you're happy with the merchandise?" said a voice in English. His German accent was not quite as heavy as Talya's had been earlier.

"I am always happy with your merchandise," responded another voice, with a less staccato phrasing. It was clear they spoke two separate languages and had landed on English in which to do business. "She is beautiful. She will suit."

"And a bit exotic, with the green eyes."

I looked at Talya, and she nodded. AnaSophia had green eyes. Apparently she was the "merchandise" being bought.

"I'm still not sure why you do this," said the first voice.

"Why I pretend to marry them?" the other laughed. "You don't know much about women, my friend. How much more willingly these young religious girls do what they're told if they think you've played by the rules. How much more they're worth if they think they have some kind of status."

"Let's get this done," was the response. "Get her now. She's had enough time to get ready."

"The bathroom," Talya whispered. "That guy was standing outside the bathroom."

As we quickly turned to go back to the chalet, the thin nervous guy reappeared behind us on the enclosed terrace. We silently changed direction and crept along the back wall to the other side of the building. There, an outdoor café sat empty, chairs vacant, awaiting the next day's patrons. Beyond it was the door back into the chalet; from there, the path continued on around the building and down the twists and turns from the ridge to the parking lot.

Talya pointed out the large windows from the men's and women's restrooms. They were frosted and had heavy metal bars. Not an exit. We'd have to get AnaSophia out through the inner door. Past the guard.

"Listen," I said. "We need a plan. My job will be to distract the guard guy. Your job, no matter what else is happening, is to grab AnaSophia and get away. Get down to the parking lot. I'll join you as soon as I can."

She nodded assent. "Just out of curiosity, how are you going to do that?"

And I realized: distract the guard guy. Another

million-dollar sentence. How would I do it? Ask him to help me move something heavy? Run in and say we saw a girl running down the hill—even though there were bars on the outside of the washroom window? If I did that, he'd run outside right to the pathway where Talya and AnaSophia would need to make their escape.

There seemed only one choice.

"I'm going to have to knock him out," I said.

She looked at me like that was a perfectly fine idea and headed inside.

As we came to the hall with the elevator to our right and the restrooms to the left, Talya's shoulders went back, she added a bounce to her walk, and she flounced her hair back. "It'll just take me a teeny sec," she said pertly to me.

I looked at my watch, playing along. "We're already late! Come *on!*"

The huge guy didn't realize where she was going until she'd pushed past him into the ladies' room.

"Hey!" he said. But she didn't stop. The door swung closed behind her.

"Girls," I said, shaking my head. "Well, I might as well take the opportunity." And I walked past him to the men's room. He turned to watch me. The minute he turned back around, I stopped, spun toward him, and walked up behind him. I knew I only had a split second of surprise before he would sound the alert and likely hurt me in very unpleasant ways.

I'd never done anything like this and sure would have liked a trial run.

But that wasn't an option, and this was my two seconds.

I sprung open my ring, threw my right arm around his shoulder, shoved the ring onto the left side of his neck, and pushed the button. He roared like an injured bull, and I came flying up off the ground as he flailed and spun back toward me. It took all my strength to hold it by his neck for the second it took to inject the knockout drug.

He flung me away and put his hand to his neck, furious. How long did this stuff take to work?

I wasn't hurt, but there's something shocking to the system about being thrown through the air and landing hard on the ground.

He looked at me with a murderous gaze as he collapsed to his knees, and then, finally, fell flat. How long had all this taken? Three seconds? It felt like an eternity.

I pounded on the door to the women's washroom.

"Let's go!" I said.

It swung open, and Talya came out, leading—perhaps dragging would be a better word—another young woman behind her. The girl was younger than Talya and was wearing an eye-popping ensemble. Her dress was white with intricate patterns of green and pink; the design on the top made it look like a vest, and a full skirt came out from a fitted waist. Multicolored trim went around the end of the sleeves, the waist, and the bottom of the dress. She was wearing pink silk pants and a pink and green long headscarf, which I later found out was called a chador. It went down nearly to the hem of the dress. Seeing her being towed in the wake of Talya, in her blue and red dirndl, made me laugh at the incongruity of being involved in a costumed rescue atop a Bavarian mountain ledge.

Of course, I was still in lederhosen.

Talya didn't take time for introductions. She nodded at me so that AnaSophia would know I was on the approved list, and the two of them headed for the exit door to start down the path to the parking lot.

I took a deep breath, feeling pretty good about my first knock-out-a-really-big-guy rescue as I hurried behind them.

But just before I got to the outer door, figures came from the right, from the side of the chalet that went up the mountain. One man grabbed Talya and shoved her to the ground. AnaSophia cried out as the other roughly took her by the arm and pulled her away.

A roar of anger escaped my mouth as I ran out the door and looked to the right, just in time to see AnaSophia disappearing, in the clutches of the tall German man, along the rock pathway up the mountain.

CHAPTER TWENTY-TWO

On the Edge

A SHORTER MAN, in a black suit with white shirt buttoned up and a black tie, stood over Talya, looking perplexed. It seemed like he thought he should stop me.

It seemed like maybe I should stop him.

Domino fifteen.

With a sigh, I switched into martial arts mode. I didn't want to kill him or anything, but I did need to slow him down. I did a spinning hook kick to the stomach to knock the air out of him and easily held his shoulders while looping his feet out from under him. He fell with a cry of alarm, like I'd broken his legs or something. It seemed he wasn't big on hand-to-hand combat.

I left him on the ground and headed up the mountain. Talya was close behind me.

"You're pretty good," she said, sounding completely surprised.

In my mind, I glared a hole straight through her. *Say that when we're outta here.*

Then the cloud enfolded us. We went from sun into netherworld. Couldn't see a hand in front of my face. Criminy. I stood stock-still and stopped Talya. We listened.

There was nothing for a second, and then a small cry, presumably from AnaSophia as she was pulled up the rocky path. Then *they* stopped. And waited.

We waited.

There was a rustling. At some point, he had to realize there was nothing for them up the mountain. And the only way back down was past us.

I turned to Talya, close behind me, mimed grabbing someone and pointed down. She nodded.

We waited silently.

A minute passed.

And then another.

The stillness was excruciating.

Finally, he decided we weren't coming.

We heard the two of them together take a tentative step down the mountain path. And then another.

They began walking for real. I thought we had them.

Then the tall man spoke, in accented English. It wasn't a monotone, but it was unconcerned. "I know you're out there," he said. "Here is the only deal I offer you. I have this girl. She is mine. I brought her here, and she will leave with me. If you try to take her from me, I will kill her. It's that simple. And then I will do the same to you. If you leave now, run down to the parking lot and disappear, she will live and so will you. But if at any time you try to stop me, you have killed her."

And he began walking, bringing her with him, at a controlled pace down toward the chalet. I had just enough time to wonder, Do speeches like that ever work? Seriously? Does anyone ever think, *Well, I was going to try to save the girl's life, but if you put it that way . . . ?*

They weren't going very quickly, as it was hard to see even the rocky ground below your feet. As he and AnaSophia moved down, Talya and I communicated silently and moved over to one side.

And then they were right above us.

As they moved past, I hung back, waiting to position myself to attack from behind, as I'd done with the bodyguard outside the restroom. I briefly wondered if, by any chance, there was another dose of the knockout drug inside my ring. Had he said anything about there being more than one?

I'd already begun to move out of the cloud toward them when I saw it.

He had a gun.

It was a small handgun, of a size to be easily concealed in a pocket or waistband.

Now it was pointed at AnaSophia's head.

What now? If I surprised him, if I grabbed him from behind, it could cause him to shoot, either from spite or from surprise.

Oh, crap.

This is usually the point in television crime dramas when the good guys throw down their weapons. Not that I had one.

But just as I was thinking I had to stay hidden and move away, there was this funny yodeling sound that bounced off the mountains. It was really loud, and really close. If I was startled, he was flabbergasted. In the split second that his gun hand went slack and he looked around, Talya came hurtling out from beside us like a banshee, hit the ground, and rolled into him. Hard.

And he tripped.

The gun went off.

Then it went flying.

Talya grabbed AnaSophia and pulled her, hard, down the mountain and out of sight of those of us still in the cloud.

Suit Man roared and clambered to his feet. This time, I hit him from behind, sending him rolling forward. I realized, with something close to panic, that I'd have to incapacitate this dude or we'd never get away. Maybe I'd need to break his leg.

I didn't think I could bring myself to break his neck.

Then he looked at me with a stare filled with fury, and I realized the choice might not be mine.

Unlike our prospective groom down the mountain, this guy knew how to fight.

I got up, trying to reposition myself and, hopefully, to see where the gun had landed. But before I was fully upright, he had my ankle. With both his hands. I tried to move forward, but he brought me down onto my knees, facing away from him, up the mountain.

Not good.

I tried to kick him off with my free foot, and I hit his shoulder, hard. He didn't let go.

I kicked again. I flipped over onto my back, and, as

he attempted to climb on top of me to knock me out, I kneed him in the jaw.

Apparently, this hurt.

Not enough to stop him.

But enough to make him really, really mad.

I tried to pull myself up, out from underneath him. He figured this out and collapsed down, onto my chest.

With all the strength I had, I pushed him over, and ended up on top. As he brought his knee up to kick me, I was able to roll to the left, putting the weight of my knees on the ground.

But my objective wasn't to get free, it was to keep this guy from heading down the mountain to get Talya and AnaSophia.

How? How?

And then I saw, on the stone behind me, the dark outline of the guy's gun.

Should I grab it? Could I shoot him?

If he disarmed me and got it himself, I was dead. I knew that.

I grabbed the gun. It was small and compact, black, with a silver grip. The safety was already off.

I took a stance, pointed it at his left leg, and pulled the trigger. There was a loud report, and I staggered a step back.

He howled with anger and pain.

And then I flung the gun away from me, toward the edge of the mountain. Apparently, not far enough. We both heard it hit the ground.

The man beneath me was up. Even though I'd shot him. It had been a clean shot, gone right through. He was bleeding, but not profusely.

He apparently decided that, wounded as he was, his best chance to retrieve his property involved retrieving his firearm. He lurched back into the cloud to the right as we faced up the mountain.

Did I need to follow him? Or could I just make a run for it?

Unfortunately, it seemed completely likely that, even if he couldn't follow us down the path, he'd have a clear shot at us from up here, at several points, if he managed to find his gun.

Domino sixteen.

I followed him up into the cloud.

I'd hurled the gun off to our right as we climbed, and that was the direction in which the blood trail headed. My whole plan was to reach the gun first, send it flying off the mountain, and hightail it out of there.

Unfortunately, this guy was determined. And fast.

Instead of heading straight up the gravel path, he'd

taken an offshoot that went off to the right. It went over a small rise, and continued on. The path itself was not straight, and rocks came shooting out to make fun-house stairs up and down as I picked through the clouds. I heard him continuing on in a labored way, with an occasional intake of breath as he stumbled. If only the cloud would part enough that I could see where he was going!

And then there was a giant step down. I hopped it and found myself on a cross-shaped ledge of concrete with a black pipe sticking up out of it. This seemed like it would be the very edge of the mountain, but the gunman was hurrying on. He took a large step down, and then another. He was in pain, but that was not at all his overriding emotion.

He was going to retrieve his property.

I followed him down onto the concrete and looked forward. He had climbed onto another cement outcropping, this one diamond shaped, and at an angle pointing up into the sky.

The gun had landed there. He picked it up and turned around.

I could tell by the crazed look in his eye that I didn't matter at all. In his mind, I was already dead. Collateral damage.

There was no time to stop, even for a second. In the time it took him to raise the weapon, I had hurled myself off the first ledge, straight onto him.

We both sprawled backward with an "oomph." The gun, and his gun arm, were pinned between us. You get to know someone in an oddly intimate way when the two of you are fighting to the death. I knew he was angry. I knew he was impatient to kill me and get on with things, because that was the only logical outcome. To do that, he needed to get up.

With all his strength, he shoved me to his left. We rolled together. It was enough that the gun moved a little. I knew it wouldn't take much for him to be able to position it in such a way that he could shoot me in the chest or abdomen at point-blank range. That couldn't happen.

Angrily I kneed him near the groin and rose up onto my knees, grabbing his gun arm with both my hands. I hit his hand down onto the pavement again and again, until his fingers gave way and the gun flew. It landed maybe three feet away, just beyond our reach.

I leapt up and grabbed it, then I flung it, this time as far away as I could.

Neither of us could hear it land. It was gone.

But he was madder than ever. He stood up and flew

toward me. There was a large circle of cement near the edge of our man-made ledge, and I sidestepped it, trying to avoid him. He used it as a springboard for his one good leg to push off and land right in front of me.

He grabbed me with both hands and began pushing me backward.

I lost my balance. The ledge was at an angle, and it was covered with loose gravel. I was less than a foot from the edge.

It was at that very moment that the clouds parted. The September sun burst through. The entire world was illuminated.

Time shattered into moments.

I could see for a hundred miles in every direction.

I could see mountain peaks and pristine lakes. And I could somehow feel as well as see the never-ending drop that toyed with me, ruffling my hair, pulling at my back, one step behind me.

Somehow, miraculously, I forced myself sideways. The gunman and I would have had equal footing, except for the fact he had been shot through the leg. He couldn't stand on it.

I had one moment, one moment only, in which I had to choose. Did I push him, with everything I had, send him flying off the mountain, into space, to certain death?

If not, there would be only one instant before he grounded the foot of his bad leg against the round slab and pushed me off.

Could I kill a man?

Even this man?

Within seconds, one of us would be losing our balance. One of us would be dropping through the thin, cold air to a certain death.

Unless . . . unless there was more than one dose in my ring. If I chose to find out, I would lose the momentary advantage I had. If there was no other dose, if I had used it all up, he would have time to push me.

He did not have any scruples at all about sending me hurtling into space.

I screamed, loud, and I grabbed him, shoving my fist into his neck. I pushed the spring-loaded button. And I waited to see which one of us had the next move.

CHAPTER TWENTY-THREE

Pockets

He grabbed his neck and looked at me, like we had a pact here, to fly off the mountain, to die, one or the other.

Instead, he crumpled to his knees and onto the ground.

I stood there staring at him as he lost consciousness.

The ring had two frigging doses.

It was only then I began to shake.

I don't know what made me stop and stoop down by him, but I did. Perhaps because I realized that once I left this mountain, I wasn't coming back.

I methodically went through his pockets. There wasn't much. I wondered if I should take his wallet, but instead took a snap of his driver's license, leaving the wallet for the authorities to find. I then took a snap of his face for facial recognition.

There were car keys in the pocket of his trousers. There was a folded brochure/program in the larger pocket of his suit coat. I grabbed it, stood, and looked at it in the brightness of the afternoon sun. Was it anything useful?

On the front was a photo of a group of girls posed together in a semicircle, like a singing group. It took only a glance for me to tell that they were in the same style tunic and pants as the girls I had followed from Afghanistan. It was a program for their concert tonight.

It opened into three panels. Along the center panel was a listing of the songs they'd sing. Each of the two side panels held photos of the individual girls. Instead of a name or a bio (what would it say, really?) was a QR code, one of those squiggly boxes that led to an Internet site.

I stuffed the program into my pocket and began to pick my way back across the cement outcroppings and down the mountain path. Now, free of cloud cover, the mountains formed a Technicolor cyclorama

surrounding the Kehlsteinhaus. As I approached the
chalet, I waited briefly to the side to see if there was
any movement there. There was none. My best guess
was that the wealthy groom/customer had gone inside
to find out where his knocked-out bodyguard was, and
that the employee who was holding unauthorized after-
hours events up here had hightailed it away.

I hurried along the back terrace and continued past
the house itself, onto the path that became the wide
walking path down the mountain. I jogged down that
as quickly as I could, making allowances for the gravel
footing, the angle, and the twists and turns. It went on
forever. Of course, the elevator went up the equivalent
of forty stories, and that was a straight shot.

I caught up with Talya and AnaSophia just before the
final turn to the parking lot. Talya had that determined
look in her eye. AnaSophia was what I would call
resigned. At best. She was a few inches shorter than
Talya, looked several years younger than either of us,
had an oval face defined by large green eyes and black
crescent eyebrows, smoky eyelashes that went on forever,
and a mouth that undoubtedly would be lovely if she
were smiling. Which she wasn't.

As we reached the parking lot, a small car went
roaring past. The wayward employee?

No one else was there when we turned the corner to assess the situation, so we hurried to our car. I jumped into the driver's seat, and Talya pulled her friend with her into the backseat.

I didn't care about anything else, didn't want to know about anything else. I just wanted to get us to safety. I pulled out of the parking lot, gunning the engine to get away from there, from that single winding road through mountain tunnels, on which we could be stopped by bad guys, by local cops, by Girl Scouts selling Tagalongs. Please God, get us out. And away.

The road, now devoid of even tour buses, was not hard to negotiate; in fact, it was much easier than driving on a straighter road at 170 miles an hour back in Springfield. The shudder of the car at those speeds, and my terror of hitting loose gravel and going flying, still held a visceral memory for me, and I gripped the steering wheel of the BMW coupe, slowing down as we rounded a curve with yet another stunning view off the mountain.

My blood was still racing as we passed the parking lot and gift shop where tourists boarded buses up to Eagle's Nest, and we joined the flow of normal traffic.

I fumbled for the controls to the navigation system,

and then for "recently found." It was there. Alouette, the restaurant. The safe house. I hit "go."

I'd expected Talya to pepper me with questions. I'd expected us to be excited and happy. Instead, she was in the backseat, arguing and speaking imploringly in Pashto with AnaSophia, who was crying. Sobbing was more like it.

"What's wrong?" I finally yelled.

"She's freaked out," Talya answered.

"Yeah. I got that."

"She thinks she was about to be married and we stopped it."

"She had been bought! You can't legally marry a fourteen-year-old girl in Germany—anywhere in Europe! Doesn't she understand that?"

"She's just afraid—afraid she's going to be sent back to Afghanistan. After her parents paid so much and took such a risk. She was promised a job. She was promised an education, if she wanted one. A rich husband was more than she had hoped for, and that's what it seemed like she was getting."

I had no answer. Why was everything so complicated? And what should happen now? Just go back and turn up with them at the safe house? After doing what

I was told not to do? After leaving two drugged guys back up at Kehlsteinhaus? *Really* bad guys who should be arrested. It seemed we should call the cops, at the very least.

Meanwhile, to the crying girl.

I fumbled in my pocket for the music program. "Here. See what you think about this."

Talya took it and opened it up.

"This is tonight's program," she said. Then she saw the photos and the QR codes. "Give me your phone."

When she had it, she found the app and scanned the box by one of the girls.

"Oh, no," she said. "Pull over. Anywhere. You've got to look at this."

We were driving past some quaint Bavarian town. It wasn't too hard to pull over and let the car idle. "Don't unlock the doors," she said.

What? I looked at the girl next to her, face tear stained and desperate. Oh.

Next thing I knew, Talya was clambering over the console into the front passenger seat of the car. She showed me the Web page that the code in the program had taken her to. It showed a girl in the program, in various happy poses. Smiling. Laughing. Working in a kitchen. Singing with the group. And, finally, in her underwear, with a number range underneath her.

"That's the price they think she'll go for," Talya breathed. "It's like an auction at Christie's, only with human beings."

"Then we were right to get AnaSophia away from them, even if she isn't happy with us at the moment."

Talya looked at me like I was crazy, or completely missing the point.

And I knew what she was going to say.

"Oh, no," I said. "No. No."

And I pulled back out into traffic.

CHAPTER TWENTY-FOUR

Plans

As I DROVE, the speaker from the center console crackled to life. "Hello, Colt." It was Supervisor Reese. Who had told me not to go. On whom I'd hung up.

"Hello, sir."

"We were able to identify the man in the recognition scan you sent."

"You were?"

"Yes. Ernst Hoth. Not a nice type. Number two man of one of the largest high-end human-trafficking rings."

"High end?"

"Yes. Specialty placements, they call them. Most

human trafficking involves smuggling people like they're freight. Dozens at a time, across borders, in cargo holds of ships, and the like. Doesn't matter if a few die in transit. But the ring Hoth works for does placements. Probably makes more for one well-dressed guaranteed virgin than for a dozen sweatshop slaves."

"He didn't seem like a nice guy," I said.

"You ran into him in person?"

"You could say that."

"Where is he now?"

"Knocked out at the top of Eagle's Nest. Along with the bodyguard of his client. Could you get someone up there?"

"We'll take care of it," he said. "You handled that by yourself?"

I glanced over. "Talya helped me. We freed AnaSophia, who was being sold separately."

"Well done."

"By the way, I don't think anyone told me my ring had more than one dose of knockout drug. That would have been useful information. How many more do I have?"

"It had more than one?" asked Reese. "That's unusual."

In other words, don't count on using it again.

"Tell him," Talya said, waving the program in my face.

"Are you heading back to the safe house?" the supervisor asked.

"*Tell him!*" she hissed, purposely loud enough to be heard.

"Tell me what?" Reese asked.

"I found a program for the girls' concert in Hoth's pocket," I explained. "There are codes by each girl that take you to a Web site with more photos. And an estimated price range."

"I'm not surprised," was all he said.

"Can you call the police, or something, to stop them? We have a place and a time and we know what's really going on."

There was silence at the other end. Then, "Where and when is the concert?"

"It's at eight o'clock," said Talya. "In the Singers' Hall at Schloss Neuschwanstein."

Another silence.

"Supervisor Reese, can't we just have the local police meet them there and arrest them?"

There was a sigh. "Technically, we could send the local police in. But one of two things would happen. Either the traffickers would immediately disable those

Web sites and hide their true intent, or they'd be arrested and all the girls would go into the system and be shipped back to Afghanistan, likely to face punishment for leaving the country with no plans to return."

AnaSophia sniffed in the back.

"Is there nothing, then, that *we* can do?" I asked. "I mean FALCON?"

Another deep sigh. "If Hoth is involved, there's a chance we might reel in Phelan, the Big Fish. Let me see who I can pull in. And what arrangements I can make for the girls before we send in the local police. But three hours isn't long to set this all up. Where are you?"

He answered that himself, as he was following our car on his screen. "You're almost back to the A8. Which means, if you keep going west rather than heading back north toward Munich, you can reach Schloss Neuschwanstein in about two and a half hours."

"Us? Why?"

"We need someone inside, to be our eyes and ears until we've got the raid in place."

"And there's no one else closer?" *Or more experienced?*

"No one we can spare." *I need the experienced agents to pull this off.*

Domino seventeen.

"How do we get there?" I asked. But Talya was

already, happily, resetting the destination in the GPS. "And how do I get in?"

"See what you can figure out. We'll be in touch."

"Sir," I said, catching him before he signed off, "will Colin be around to talk to sometime?"

"He'll be around sometime. Can't guarantee when."

And he was gone.

I clutched the wheel and stared straight ahead, trying to sort through my thoughts.

The good news: I wasn't fired. In fact, I was more in than I had been. Further good news: Reese was seeing about getting us backup. And contacting local authorities.

Bad news: I had to figure out how to get into an auction of girls for sale by myself. Without getting caught.

Really, how hard could it be?

CHAPTER TWENTY-FIVE

Hohenschwangau

So I'd gone from not feeling secure pulling out of a Chinese restaurant in Springfield to being Mr. Autobahn in a matter of days. Talya informed me there was no legal speed limit on those German highways. You were permitted to drive at a speed safe for current conditions. If you crashed, you were ticketed, because obviously you were driving too fast for those conditions.

Still, after the adventures with my mom, eighty-five seemed like a Sunday drive.

Pre-driver, indeed.

Somehow, thinking of Springfield brought me to

thoughts of Malin James, the girl I liked from afar. I remembered her smile and wished she could see me shooting down the road. I had the feeling she wouldn't be either crying in the backseat or egging me on in the front seat. She'd have common sense. We could talk things out.

But here I was. And not with Malin. "What town are we going to?" I asked.

"Hohenschwangau."

"Oh. Glad I asked."

"The town doesn't matter! We're going to Schloss Neuschwanstein. The castle."

"They're singing in a castle?"

"Only, like, the most famous one in the world. The big white one, up in the mountains of Bavaria. Built by King Ludwig II. The Swan King. Or 'Mad King Ludwig,' although there's doubt that he was actually crazy. Ring a bell?"

I'd obviously been studying the wrong part of the world. I shook my head.

"You've been there?" I asked her.

How could you stay in this part of the world and not visit Neuschwanstein Castle?

"Ludwig was a dreamer who loved the arts. He grew up in a castle with walls painted with murals of hero tales. Became king of Bavaria after his father died suddenly when Ludwig was eighteen. It was bad timing for a newbie, because within the next five years there were two wars, which resulted in Kaiser Wilhelm making Bavaria part of a German state, ruled by him. So Ludwig, who was really rich, created his own kingdom where he could be the kind of pure king in the Arthurian legends. He built incredible castles and supported the composer Richard Wagner, who wrote sweeping operas about all these legends.

"The cool thing about the castles is that they were built long after castles needed to be fortresses to ward off enemies. He built his to fairy tale specifications; in fact, Ludwig hired an opera set designer to plan Neuschwanstein."

"He built all these castles with Bavaria's money?"

"No. With his own funds. But toward the end of his life, he was so into castle mania that he ran out of money and borrowed a lot. Tried to strong-arm his cabinet into persuading other monarchs to lend him personal funds. Finally, the government had him declared insane, arrested him—in Neuschwanstein Castle—and took him to another castle, where he died under mysterious circumstances the very next day."

"The irony is, of course, that since his death, Ludwig's

spectacular castles have been a huge tourist draw for Bavaria. They've paid for themselves many times over."

"And, I take it, you can rent the Singers' Hall."

"It can't be cheap," Talya said. "And these guys must have disguised their true purpose really well. But makes sense, if you pride yourself on high-end auctions, to do them somewhere extravagant."

There was something I wanted to ask Talya but was afraid to in front of AnaSophia. I didn't know if she might understand any English. It struck me that we hadn't heard from her for a while, so I glanced into the backseat. AnaSophia was stretched out.

"Is she *asleep*?" I asked, incredulous.

How could you be asleep so soon after being saved from being bought as a slave? Or having a fake wedding in country that was not your own?

Talya heard the question within my question.

"We've been fed so many downers lately that it will take a while for them to get out of her system. I think it was only adrenaline that got her down to the car. If I hadn't palmed half my pills, I'd be back there with her right now."

"So. If we can't rescue these girls, what happens to them?"

"The short answer is, they simply disappear. And no one ever sees them again."

"But where are they really?"

Talya's voice got quiet. "You don't want to know."

I looked over at her. I did want to know.

"They're slaves. Whoever buys them can do anything they want with them and not be held accountable. They can be used as household slaves, work slaves, sex slaves. They can even be tortured and killed, and no one would ever know. No one would ever care. Although if you pay this much for someone, you're probably not looking for factory help. That's all I'll say."

"But the girls themselves don't know this?"

"No. They've been told they have wonderful things ahead. Often poor girls are promised restaurant work in a foreign land. But these girls, who all come from comparatively wealthy families, have been promised adoption by very rich families. Good finishing schools. Well-arranged marriages. And, after spending time with them, I'll tell you that, because they're being presented as singers, many of them are hoping for careers as international pop stars."

"Seriously? But that's crazy. Nobody gets to be an international pop star! Well, except Katy Perry." I remembered to whom I was speaking. I blushed. "And you. Of course, you."

Talya burst into laughter. While I was completely embarrassed, it did lighten the mood.

"I know, I know. You don't think of me as a star. You think of me as a really annoying co-spy."

"Agent."

I didn't want to tell her how close to the truth she'd come. The annoying part, anyway. But as far as I was concerned, she wasn't actually a co-anything.

We got off the highway and began winding through mountains and past cobalt-blue lakes. This whole place looked art directed. Yellows, golds, and reds of autumn leaves made me feel like we'd wound up in some fairy tale book. It was too stunning to be actual scenery.

And then, as we got close to Hohenschwangau, I saw it. Perched up on a mountain, outlined by a magnificent Alpine sunset in purples and oranges. Neuschwanstein Castle.

Of course I recognized it when I saw it. It was the castle on which Disney had based Sleeping Beauty's Castle at Disneyland. Only better. King Ludwig had out-Disneyed Disney.

It had soaring walls and turrets and towers and windows. Rather than being all stone and brown and crumbling like a good medieval castle should be, it was white and blue and shimmering. It was the ultimate fairy tale castle, brought to life.

We came into town on a long, tree-lined road, which soon was populated by restaurants, parking lots, gift shops, a hotel, and many, many tourists.

The concert started at eight. Did that mean the girls were there now, up in the castle? Which would mean the bad guys were also there now? The prospective buyers would start coming in very soon.

I was suddenly nervous about the girl in the backseat. What if one of the bad guys saw her?

"I'm not so sure we should be driving around here with AnaSophia," I said. "Just how do I get into this castle? Is there some kind of back door? Or basement entrance?"

"It's not going to be easy," said Talya. "The castle is built on a mountain ledge. The walls are sheer drops on every side except the one with the front courtyards and entrances. And there's only one road that goes up there. There's really only one way in."

"How do we find out what's going on?"

"It's going to be tough," she said. "It's a long way up. You have to either hike—and it's much farther than the path down from Eagle's Nest—or you take one of the horse carts up. But they stop running when the castle closes for the day."

The road split, and I paused beside the rounded end of a picturesque hotel. Before I could express my exasperation at having to hike up yet another mountain, Talya had leapt from the vehicle. She ran across the cobblestoned street to where a man was sitting on the driver's plank of a horse-driven cart. Not surprisingly, he was dressed a lot like me at the moment. But of course, it was his job to be Bavarian and picturesque.

Talya spoke with him, enthusiastically, for several minutes. She was doing the little bounce she did when she was flirting information out of someone. The horse-cart driver was answering her questions; when he ran out of answers, she looked really concerned. He scratched his head and gave her some sort of suggestion.

Then he shrugged, and she smiled, and she came and got back into the car.

"So, what's up?" I asked.

"He said the castle has been closed to the public for an hour. He just made his last trip back down. He also said whoever has it rented out for the night has heavy security. The final road to the castle itself is closed, unless you have identification and an invitation."

"Which we don't."

"How do we get you in? This is going to be harder than I thought. We could try the scaffolding they're using to redo the outside, but it might be hard to get down to the bottom of the ravine so we could climb it to start with. I'm fairly sure the scaffolding is meant to be accessed from the top, not the bottom, so it might not even be reachable to climb."

I said, "First, I'm not climbing a fifty-story scaffold, even if it's reachable. Second, I don't think we should be sitting here in the car in the middle of the village, when there are only two roads through town and someone might recognize AnaSophia."

"I know, I know. I'm thinking. He also said the concertgoers are dressed in formal attire."

"Formal attire?"

"Evening jackets. Tuxedoes. Come on. I know where we're going in the meantime."

"Where?"

"To the friends Thorne and I stayed with when we were here. We can get AnaSophia safely tucked away and figure out how to get you in there."

We continued on, turning right on Alpseestrasse. We soon passed beneath the town's original castle, Castle Hohenschwangau, which soared on a promontory above us. Apparently Ludwig's father had it built. It seemed to me that Ludwig probably grew up thinking that's what kings did—they built castles overlooking lakes in the mountains. Although it also seemed that one castle per town would probably do.

The road was named for the huge lake, Alpsee, as you left town to the west.

As we drove, I checked in with Supervisor Reese once more, hopeful they'd already gotten someone inside. No dice. And he said they still needed someone in the castle to let them know where everyone was and what was going on. They didn't want it to turn into a hostage situation; that would be a nightmare for all involved. He assured me they were pulling the raid together as quickly as possible.

He also had no idea of how I should get in. His focus was obviously elsewhere.

"Colt, be careful. These are dangerous people, professionals. If they find out who you are, they will kill you as soon as look at you. If you weren't the only person we have on site, we'd never send you in. But it's already nearly concert time. I'm not completely sure we're going to be able to get in there and extract these girls as it is. So don't do anything stupid. If you can't get in, you can't get in. The last thing we want is to tip them off that a raid is coming."

Talya pointed to a turnoff onto a private road that ran from Alpseestrasse toward the lake. I swung the car to the left as I hung up from Supervisor Reese.

The set of her jaw told me that she didn't care for his comment about not being sure we could get in there to save everybody.

To Talya, saving these girls was personal.

Failure was not an option.

CHAPTER TWENTY-SIX

Schwan Haus

WE DROVE A long way through old-growth forest before rounding a curve to see the manor house before us. I'm not certain, in correct European terms, that it actually was a manor house, but it was gorgeous. It was four stories of white stone, in French provincial style. The center section was rounded, with balconies that ran the full length of each floor. My guess was it had been built in the 1600s or 1700s.

Talya pointed me to the front of the house, where a circular drive led to large doors flanked by topiaries.

Half a dozen cars were parked, nose out, to one side of a center garden.

"Shall I wait in the car?" I said, almost hopefully. Usually, I don't know people who live in mansions. Or nobility, which you'd have to be to own something like this.

"Come on," she said. "Let me introduce you."

"How do you know they're home?" I hissed as we got out of the car.

"I recognize Robert's Lamborghini," she said.

Yep, a white Lamborghini was parked against the stone wall.

There was a doorbell, which she pushed, although the door swung open so quickly I was fairly certain they had some sort of early warning system when cars approached the house.

The door was answered by an actual butler. Talya smiled broadly and called him by name, launching into a stream of German. He half-smiled at her and invited us in. Then he gave a small bow and headed off to tell Robert, and whomever else, that we were here.

We stood in the entry hall, which was the size of a ballroom. A marble staircase greeted us straight ahead. It ran up to open hallways, which led in both directions, overlooking the hall below. The floors beneath us were marble, and everything else was either gold or brass or a very warm wood, giving the old-world feeling of money that mansions in the United States could never quite achieve.

We didn't have long to wait before a tall, lanky man wearing pressed trousers, a burgundy sweater, and a shirt with an open collar came striding from the direction in which the butler had disappeared.

"Talya, my love," he said, but in a way that made "my love" sound affectionate rather than affected. "What a surprise! Judy is away for the afternoon; she will be disconsolate not to be here to greet you! What on earth are you doing here?"

"I'm so sorry to impose, especially unexpectedly," she said. "But I'm in a tight spot and I was hoping you could help me out."

"Of course," he said. "You know I will. Who is your friend?"

"Colt Shore, meet Robert Edward Rich. He's a . . ." She stopped, as if she didn't know in which direction to go. "A retired history professor," she finally landed on.

Which was obviously the tiniest part of the actual story.

"Colt is . . . a drummer."

"Glad to have you," said Mr. Rich. He wore glasses, was perhaps in his sixties, but in very good shape. He seemed kind. He also seemed like you might not want to mess with him. When he spoke English, his accent was American.

As our host spoke, the front door opened, and the butler stood before us, perplexed. "Beg pardon," he said in English. "Ernst went to park the car, but there seems to be a person in it."

"Yes," Talya said, turning back to our host. "That part's what we need help with."

"This does sound interesting," said Robert. "Shall we invite your person in?"

"She's asleep," said Talya. "I need somewhere to stash her while we're off saving her friends."

"We're always happy to help when someone needs stashing," he said.

"Here's the thing. We've only now saved her, but she doesn't realize she's been saved. So we need to put her somewhere safe, where folks will keep an eye on her, so she won't make a run for it."

"Because she doesn't know she's been saved."

"Exactly."

"Well, we'd best bring her in and get her stashed," Robert said, obviously getting a kick out of Talya arriving in full spy mode. "Ernst is large; do you suppose he could do the carrying?"

"Certainly." This from the butler.

"Then why don't you see her settled in the yellow room. And ask Gretel to stay with her, to make certain she doesn't run off into the night. Meanwhile, let me conclude my business call. Come join me in the library once . . . what is her name?"

"AnaSophia," said Talya.

"Once AnaSophia is settled."

I thought briefly about volunteering to carry AnaSophia to her new quarters, but I quickly realized that Ernst, hefty and muscled, was the man. She roused briefly as Talya cajoled her out of the car, and looked confused as she was carried inside. I followed the three of them up the grand staircase and along winding, opulent hallways, but waited outside the door while they brought her into the yellow room. A few minutes later, Talya came out and reported that AnaSophia had let herself be put into a proper white nightgown and tucked back into bed.

Gretel, who was actually a rotund middle-aged woman and not a waif from the woods, went to sit in the room before we left.

I followed Talya back through the hallways, down

the stairs, and into the library. A fire glowed in the fireplace, and tall burnished bookcases lined the walls. They were filled with books, many of them history texts. A large window framed a view of the lake. And there, in the mountains above the town, was the castle, Neuschwanstein, where, even now, moments were ticking down until the girls each left, never to be seen again.

"So," our host said seriously, but with a glint in his eye, "from the looks of things, you're here either enjoying Oktoberfest or selling some kind of hot chocolate."

"Oh, Robert, it's a long story," Talya said. She launched into a shortened version. Part of me wondered if we should be telling so much to a stranger—but then, Robert was a stranger to me, but not to her. True, in a cruel twist, Robert could be the mastermind of the plot and could once again toss Talya and AnaSophia in for the bidding, but FALCON was all about trusting people who were trustworthy and building a base of as many allies as possible.

Talya trusted him. And she seemed to have a pretty good sense about these things.

"So we need to figure out how to get Colt into the castle. Are there any secret passages you know of?"

"I'm afraid not. There are various ways in and out once you get past the Gateway Building and the lower courtyard, but there's only one pathway that leads up there, and I'm sure they've got it covered. In fact, back in 1886, when word got out that the government was sending men to arrest King Ludwig, a local middle-aged countess heard about it. She met the half dozen guards outside the Gateway building and managed to hold them all off with an umbrella. In other words, the only entrance seems fairly easy to defend."

As he said this, he walked over to his desk in the corner and logged on to the computer.

I said, "So, although King Ludwig didn't need to build the castle to be impenetrable to catapults and such, he did a great job of making it hard for uninvited guests to get in."

"Absolutely. Sheer cliff drops on every side, and one road up, one road out."

"So there is a road out, through the kitchen."

"Yes, but it comes off the main road. And the kitchen door will undoubtedly be guarded."

He had sat down at the computer and pulled up the castle's official Web site, which was kind enough to feature blueprints of every floor of the castle.

Apparently the kitchen was on the lowest level, built into the rock of the mountain. The second floor, which had not been completed before Ludwig's arrest, was now a cafeteria and gift shop. The third floor had the large throne room, the king's bedroom, dining room, salon, study, something called a "grotto," conservatory, and servants' quarters.

The fourth and top floor held only the second floor of the throne room, with a balcony overlooking it, and the Singers' Hall. Which meant those two rooms were huge.

Robert pointed out where two circular stairways were: the larger one for the king and his guests, and the smaller one for servants that was also supposed to lead to something called the "knight's baths."

"Ludwig insisted on having all the modern conveniences, so the castle not only had hot and cold running water and flushing toilets, but it also has an elevator."

The elevator ran from the kitchen, stopping by the cafeteria on the second floor, then outside the grotto and conservatory on the third floor, and across from the Singers' Hall on the top level. Would this information come in handy? I hoped not. Frankly, I'd had enough of elevators and their shafts for one day. "The elevator is not large enough to handle the flow of tourists. They can only see the castle if they can walk the many steps from floor to floor."

"But the elevator works?" I asked.

"One would assume," Robert answered. "Schloss Neuschwanstein is a cash cow for the country. They do keep it up."

Talya gave an impatient stomp of the foot. "None of this matters if we can't get him inside!" she said.

I looked again at the online footprint of the castle. The approaching road led to the Gateway Building, which had a rectangular center section with a triangular top and circular turret buildings on each side. There was a giant gate in the center. Once you were inside, you still weren't home free—you were in a lower courtyard that faced a sheer wall. From there, you had to access a flight of stairs to the upper courtyard. It would be simple to deny people access either on the road, through the gate, or up the stairs. Three points of easy guarding that would be nearly impossible to pass.

I gave a heavy sigh. "Honestly, I don't see any way to that upper courtyard and the palace unless you jumped from a plane," I said.

"And flying planes that close to the castle is illegal," said Robert. "You'd be busted from the minute you took off from any local airport. They'd immediately see on the radar what your plane was doing."

"Not to mention, the guys on the ground would hear you coming for miles," agreed Talya.

My stomach was knotting and reknotting. The only problem was, I wasn't sure which idea was more upsetting: finding a way to get into the castle, or not finding a way.

The agents from FALCON were the pros. Did they really need to know who was in the castle and where they were and what was going on?

Even as I thought it, I realized, of course they did. Things would go much more quickly and smoothly.

And yet, if there was no way? Supervisor Reese himself had said these guys would kill you as soon as look at you. Not only that, it had come back to me where I'd heard the name Phelan, whom Reese had called the head honcho. He was the guy my mother had mentioned as the person running a huge international human trafficking ring. Who had sent men to pursue us in Springfield. To shoot at us. To kill us.

Something happened then to Talya's face. All the anxiety fell away, and she grinned.

Actually grinned.

"Robert, can you please get this guy out of these ridiculous lederhosen and into a monkey suit? He's got a concert to attend. And I know exactly how to get him inside."

CHAPTER TWENTY-SEVEN

Night Sky

WITHIN MINUTES, I was in a tuxedo and black dress shoes, Talya was in borrowed jeans, blouse, and jacket, and we were back in the M3 coupe, heading off into the night. Talya programmed an address into the GPS, and I pulled out. I guess since it was my organization's car, I got to drive. Pre-driver though I was.

She wouldn't tell me where we were going. Instead, she spent the time making me repeat, in Pashto, "I am a friend of Farrin's" (which was the name Talya had gone by in the girls' school). "I am here to help. Follow me, I will take you to safety." Admittedly, it came more easily

AGENT COLT SHORE **DOMINO 29**

since I'd spent the hours with the FALCON guy pretrip, but still, my mind was too brimming and my adrenaline was too pumping to grasp it very well. So she made me say it again. And again.

As we drove up and up the side of a mountain, she also threw in "I'm Gunter. Where do I go?" in German. Which I told her I wouldn't use, because then people would assume I spoke German and would reply to me in a language I didn't understand. But to tell you the truth, her crazy language lessons helped keep me steady and focused, and even contemplating the possibility that I might end up inside the castle.

After we'd driven higher and higher on a mountain road, she had me turn off onto a lane. We passed a brown building with a large parking lot and kept going, up a gravel path that I assumed was for walking in daylight hours. We continued up and finally emerged into a large clearing on the side of the mountain with a huge grass lawn, several open sheds, and a house on the near side.

I parked and she got out, then turned around. "Hey. Give me your money," she said.

I fumbled in my pockets and pulled out the wad of euros I had left from the teller machine at the airport. Then she ran and disappeared into the house.

I got out of the car and stood, overlooking the

breathtaking scenery before me: the surrounding mountains, the villages settled into the valley. And Neuschwanstein Castle, in the distance to my left. Taunting me.

It wasn't long before the door to the house swung open and Talya exited with a young man in his late twenties. They were arguing in German. That is, Talya was talking heatedly and every once in a while he'd argue something back. Like a question. And she'd respond. Animatedly. As if she couldn't stop, or he might say no.

In the middle of it, they walked past where I waited in evening clothes by my BMW. "This is Colt," Talya said in English, and the young man shook my hand, while he still was walking, and said, "Nice to meet you."

What happened over the next ten minutes was like a short film. The two of them walked to a long shed. The man, whose name I seemed to have purposely not been told, worked with Talya to remove something large. He and Talya continued to work together, arguing the entire time. Yet working very fast.

I sort of didn't want to know—it was kind of like people getting a death notification and thinking if they don't open the door, it won't be true—because I honestly thought, whatever they were building, that there was a real likelihood I wouldn't survive the night. I could either die or be badly injured attempting to get into the castle or being found out once I was inside.

But finally, I had to walk over and look.

The two of them had put together a very large hang glider. And straight down the mountain from it was a gigantic ramp.

I didn't know what to say. Remembering the plane, I started with, "This has to be illegal."

"Hang gliding past Neuschwanstein is not illegal. Nighttime is frowned upon. But we're stealing it," Talya said.

"I have no idea how to work one of these things," I said. "And I'm not about to learn."

"No. You're not. Remember the part about me and extreme sports? Hang gliding is my favorite. I've got the highest certification. In fact, I did many of my training flights right here. The weather is good. Well, good enough. And enough lives are at stake that we're going to give it a go. We're going to tandem glide. I'll drop you off. So to speak."

"From *where?*" I asked. "Half a mile up?"

She didn't answer. Glider Man glared at her, which led me to suspect he'd been giving her this same argument.

"I'm not going to let those girls disappear forever."

"You're willing to risk my life for theirs?"

She stopped dead and looked at me. "I thought *you* were risking your life," she said. "I'm merely trying to help you succeed."

"How will they not see us coming?"

"How would they? We're silent. It's dark out. And they're not looking up."

"How do you know that?"

Glider Man stopped, startled, like it hadn't occurred to him that I wasn't in on this.

"Are you doing this, or have you got a better idea?" Talya asked.

I had no other ideas.

"That's what I thought," she said. She went back to the shed. When she returned, she was wearing this funny sleeping bag/cape thing that went all the way down to the ground. She was also wearing a helmet and carrying another one.

"How is this going to work? The whole part about us stealing this?" I asked. Glider Man was helping her strap in to a harness that was connected to a triangular metal frame beneath a large black kite. The front of the kite was shaped like a giant arrow, which divided into two sides as it went backward.

"After our flight, if the authorities are after us for buzzing the castle or anything, I'll ditch the glider and pay to replace it. If it seems like no one is paying attention, I'm going to try to land it at Robert's. Meanwhile, I gave him gave your euros as a down payment."

"Great."

"Here is the plan. You and I take off. Jake drives our car back to Robert's. From there he walks to the village and has a drink with friends, so he can prove he wasn't up here tonight when the glider was stolen. I drop you off at the castle, land at Robert's, dismantle and stash the glider, which he picks up tomorrow after the bad guys are arrested and the girls are long gone."

"You are insane," I said. "Certifiably insane."

"So who's more insane?" she asked. "The person handing out the helmet or the guy putting it on?"

She handed me the helmet.

"There's a chance this can work?" I asked. "And a chance we won't both die?"

"Worst is, we buzz the castle, can't get low enough to drop you, and have to land without getting you in."

I took the helmet.

Domino eighteen.

"Okay," she said. "Usually, as the tandem rider, you'd be wearing the wind sock thing, but you'll be fine. We've figured out how to secure you in such a way that you can untether yourself when we're right over the castle. I'm driving. You're behind me. When the time comes and you're unsnapped, you need to completely let go and drop down without dragging me. If I crash in the courtyard, we're both toast. Got that?"

"Yes."

"Good. Leave the flying to me. You're the tourist on this flight."

We walked the remaining way to the ramp. It was wooden, very steep, and pointed down the mountain. "You know how to land and roll?" she asked.

"Why?" I asked, shocked. If you fell off the end of this ramp, there was nothing there. It was curtains.

"For when I drop you in the courtyard," she said.

"Oh. Yeah. Years of tumbling."

We stood together at the top of the ramp. Jake ran a nylon harness around me and snapped one end to the frame of the glider and the other end to Talya. He showed me where to grab her shoulders, once we took off. He showed me how to unsnap the harness as we approached Neuschwanstein.

"Now," said Talya. "We run down the ramp together. When I yell 'up,' quit running and let your legs fly up in back of you."

We moved together to the center of the ramp. Apparently, we were really doing this.

"Run *fast!*" she yelled, and we both ran with all we had.

And then the ramp was gone, and a huge cushion of air had picked us up, and we were aloft. We were flying.

It was incredible.

The moon had risen; it was nearly full.

We were crazy high up, airplane high, sailing over ancient forests and lakes that caught the reflection of the moon. Talya and I were both lying flat, and she was using her body to bank and steer. I held on to her shoulders, stretched out above her.

It was a feeling like I'd never known before. Safely tethered yet flying free. Death-defying danger wrapped in practiced safety. The moon and the mountains and the sky and the night air, and Talya.

Talya Ellis. Seriously.

Whatever happened later tonight, even if I died saving those girls, I would have this moment of awe and wonder.

Talya's hands were on the bottom of the frame, which she could manipulate to steer our hang glider. Attached to the front of the frame was a GPS.

Not that we needed one to find the castle. It was

illuminated like a beacon in the distance, urging us on.

It was fascinating to watch how Talya harnessed the wind to steer us closer and closer. No one below took any notice of us. The kite was dark. We were shadows in the sky.

As we approached the castle, my heart accelerated. Could we actually pull this off? And if we did, would people see us? Would I be grabbed immediately?

Talya took a giant sweeping circle around the top of it for reconnaissance.

My hopes were dashed. It looked impossible. The inner courtyard, undoubtedly huge in real life, left hardly any room for banking a kite and getting back out. For the first time I realized this attempted drop-off, even if successful on my end, was extremely dangerous for her. Even if she made it back up over the other wall, she could get caught on the building, or not have the right wind, and go tumbling down to her doom.

But this was not a girl who let reality dictate her actions.

As we came back around, I realized she figured we had to come in from the front. I'd have seconds to slide off, or she'd have no chance whatsoever to regain enough altitude to turn and take the wall.

Which brought me back to myself. As we approached the front gate, I clearly saw two guards, also in evening clothes, right outside the gatehouse. They were chatting to each other and laughing.

It undoubtedly seemed to them that the hard part was over and their guard duty from here on out was simple. There was another man down the path you'd have to pass to make it up to them.

Clearly, all the expected guests were inside.

The guards didn't even glance up as we sailed over the top of the gatehouse and then over the lower courtyard.

Both my snaps undone, I waited until we were maybe twenty feet above the upper courtyard. Then I let go of Talya's shoulders and gave myself a little push up and backward.

The sudden decrease in weight gave her a sudden boost, and a breeze tossed her up higher than she'd expected to go.

I couldn't watch any longer, because my future, and the pavement, was hurtling at me.

And it was going to hurt.

CHAPTER TWENTY-EIGHT

Concert

I LANDED AS gently as possible on the balls of my feet, then dropped to roll. The neat tumbling move I had envisioned was unfortunately, and immediately, cut short by the helmet on my head. So instead, I crashed to the side, my neck smarting from my head being jammed, my feet killing me from the drop, and the entire left side of my body bruised and contused while shock waves from the landing pulsed through me.

As they subsided, I lay there for a moment, trying not to moan, trying to decide if I could even stand up.

Then I thought of the guards on the path who could

possibly have seen something and be headed this way to investigate. I thought of the girls inside the castle. I had to move. I also didn't want the authorities and FALCON agents who eventually arrived for the raid to find me moaning and rolling in the courtyard.

Stretched out on my back, I undid the helmet strap and took it off. Then I rolled over onto the good side of my body and tried to stand up. It only worked if I did it in stages. Hands and knees, one knee down, one knee up, pulled to standing. Staggered across courtyard toward a very tall flight of steps.

Stashed helmet.

Looked at tall flight of stairs. Realized there's no choice. Crawled up them.

Entered door. Staggered into hallway. Staggered down hallway to circular staircase.

Looked up at stone stairs. And more stone stairs. The ones that went past the two floors that were never completed. Hundreds of stairs. Knew the Singers' Hall was on the top floor.

Knew there was no way in heaven or hell that I could climb those stairs.

Staggered back into an alcove off the hall and leaned against the wall. Looked out the tall windows, at the villages, the mountains, the lakes, the moon.

Hurt so much I felt like crying.

Nothing to do but pray. So I did. Didn't even know what for. Just help.

Heard faint sounds of music, of girls singing. Oh, crap.

My watch lit up. *Where are you?*

Why did they even ask? They had me on a screen. They knew exactly where I was.

Are you in?

I didn't answer, because I couldn't help. I was in and I couldn't help.

I heard another snatch of the music. I recognized it as the first song on the program we found at Eagle's Nest. The first song of the girls who were about to sing through a program of ten songs and then vanish.

I tried to stand up straight, and realized my biggest problems were my throbbing head and my right ankle. I didn't know if it was broken, but it hurt to put weight on it. I went out into the hall again and gazed up at the stairs.

Too late, I heard someone coming up behind me at a fast clip.

"Heinrich?"

I turned. It was a short, slim woman in a black dress and a white apron.

"Nein," I said. And—wait for it—the German version of "I am Gunter. Where do I go?"

She let off with a harangue in German, obviously put out at Heinrich, in which I, as Gunter, bore some of the blame. But I was too sore and discouraged to care.

"I'm Heinrich's American cousin. I'm sorry, but I don't speak German."

"Tell me the truth," she said, swinging into English without losing any of her anger. "Is he drunk again?"

"I don't know," I answered honestly. "But I am here."

"Come," she said. And she turned and stalked off down the corridor. It was all I could do to follow her, but I did.

Domino nineteen.

She led me straight to the elevator. While we waited for it, she looked me up and down, noticing the tux.

"Have you got a comb?" she asked.

I shook my head.

She sighed and handed me one from her pocket. I apparently had helmet hair. The comb didn't work miracles, I'm sure, but she nodded, and I followed her onto the elevator.

We went up. "Since you're dressed, I need you inside," she said. "You're going to pour the wine and champagne."

We got off on the third floor, which was Ludwig's throne room and residence. I could still hear them singing above. "Come along," she said. "We can't take the elevator up from here, it would disturb the concert."

I made the decision right then and there that no matter what, like an Olympic gymnast, even if both my ankles were broken, I would follow this woman up. We hurried along the luxurious hallway, all dark wood and huge, fantastic paintings of various legendary characters.

We turned left into the Lower Hall, vaulted hallways lined with huge, half-circle paintings of legendary Siegfried and his friends. The woman, whom I assumed was head of catering, swished past the entrance to the throne room on the right and the royal apartments to the left, and came to the stairs in the small circular tower.

She started up. "Ma'am?" I asked. If I was going to attempt to climb, I was going to do one thing to cheer myself up. "Do you have any aspirin?"

She glared at me. Her hair was brought back into a severe bun, which probably made her look meaner than she actually was.

"Why? Hangover?"

"No, ma'am. It's my ankle. I . . . turned it."

"I'll have to check, down in the kitchen," she said. And she continued up the stairs.

I followed as best I could, keeping as much weight as possible off my right ankle. Every seven or eight steps, she'd wait for me to catch up, then glare at me. I tried my best to give her a charming smile in return.

And then, finally, we were at the top. The Upper Hall was no less grand; more paintings of legendary people in Viking helmets. Immediately to our right was a small wooden door. I followed Catering Matron through.

We entered into the back of the Singers' Hall. The ceilings were vaulted wood, square panel after square panel, beam after beam. From the beams hung four of the hugest, most exquisite chandeliers ever made, each shaped as a six-petaled rose window; hundreds of candles seemed to float through space. Three matching candelabras, each standing six feet hall, ran the sides of the room. To my right was a wall with windows; to my left the wall had interior windows open to the side hall. There was one door on that wall, and the small door behind, where we'd entered. But those seemed to be the only ways in or out.

The room was filled with very comfortable concert chairs, occupied by men in tuxedoes—and, to my surprise, a half a dozen women in evening gowns.

Catering Matron slid across the back of the room with me in tow. Behind us and up three steps was an alcove where perhaps the king would sit. It had three arches, which made it resemble a triptych. Directly in front of it was a very long catering table, covered with a burgundy cloth. There were dozens of bottles of wine, red on one side, white on the other, and two champagne buckets on either end. Crystal goblets of wine stood in lines. A spread of canapés and hors d'oeuvres flanked the front of the table.

And I was suddenly famished. Not hungry, famished. We'd been through Munich, Kehlsteinhaus, and Hohenschwangau since I'd last eaten. I realized that harder than climbing stairs on my bad ankle would be not touching the cheese sticks.

"There will be an intermission," she said. "You are the only one dressed appropriately, so you will have to pour. You may offer some of the Spätburgunder already poured; a bit of the Riesling just as the break begins. But pour no sparkling wine until it is requested."

I nodded. There was another young guy there, probably in his early twenties. He was wearing black pants and a white golf shirt, which, apparently, was fine for working in the kitchen but for serving, not so much. She motioned to him and he trotted out of the room behind her.

Before I could orient myself, she was back, a long

white apron in hand. In an expert move, she slung it around my waist under my tuxedo jacket and tied it. It nearly reached the ground. She looked me up and down. And again, she was gone.

And then, fighting off the urge to empty the platters of their funny-looking finger foods and doing my best to ignore the throbbing in my head and occasional double vision, I dared look ahead into the room. To see what was really going on.

First, there were the girls. They were singing in the front of the room. Somehow, I hadn't let myself fully engage. When I did, I got almost a physical jolt. They were beautiful. Each one. Oh, I'm not talking about delicate facial features or a curvaceous figure, but as they sang, each one nearly glowed. Each thought she was *this close* to a future in the promised land. None had any idea her life as a free person was about to end.

Each wore a colorful formal dress, the kind AnaSophia had been in for her wedding. The outfit included silk pants and a chador on her head. To broadcast her modesty. To raise her price.

Only then did I allow myself to surreptitiously look at what was going on in the room. People weren't exactly smiling and clapping to the music. Instead, they were barely listening. They were each on a handheld device, some on their phones, some on small tablets. The man in front of me had a BlackBerry and a stylus. He was going back and forth between photos. I couldn't tell if they were photos of the same girl or if he was comparison shopping.

Two men stood by the door to the interior hallway. I recognized one as the man who had shepherded the choir out of Afghanistan. He had a long face, a long, rectangular nose, and his skin was pocked from former scars. I didn't think there was any way he could recognize me or have gotten any incriminating description of me from his cohort at Eagle's Nest.

My watch buzzed again. "148215." *Are you there and free to communicate?*

I exhaled a breath I didn't know I'd been holding and responded: "229713." All clear.

I held the watch up close, as if squinting for the time, and said, "I'm in the concert. Top floor. Singers' Hall. All girls here. Clients and guards also."

The answer, in text, was, "Is this guy there?"

There came a photo of distinguished gentleman with blondish-brown hair. His face was oval, mustache and beard that were blond with touches of brown and gray. You could tell from his headshot that he would be wearing an expensive suit.

I scanned the men in the room, looking for him. No dice. I hit the *N*.

"That's the top boss, Kenneth Phelan. We didn't really expect him to show up at an auction; it's too dangerous."

What Reese didn't add was that anyone with the chutzpah to rent out the Singers' Hall for a concert that violated international law might not really care about the dangerous part. Conversely, he might be smart enough to stay a step removed.

"How about guards? How many and where?"

"Three outside the Gateway Building. None on the third floor, right below this one."

"How about up on four?"

I thought I'd remembered seeing one at the other end of the hallway by the large stairs when Catering Matron had dragged me up the small stairs. But intelligence like this was why they needed me inside. The number of guards was the sixty-four-thousand-dollar question.

How could I find out?

I peered into one of the champagne buckets and shook it a little, as if unhappy with the amount of ice. Then I removed the bottles, set them on the table, took the bucket, and limped out the back doorway into the hall.

The large hall was empty at that moment. Taking a deep breath, I hobbled down it, straight toward the main circular staircase, peered down it, and turned back around all before noticing that the five men in the side hall had shoved their hands inside their tuxedo jackets and started toward me.

I looked up, as if innocent and really surprised, raised my eyebrows, and lifted the cooler.

They all stopped. The lead guy, obviously the boss, came up, peered into the ice, and motioned me back down the hall with an irritated gesture.

I gave him a "what's *your* problem?" look that I imagined would have come from Gunther. I was 100 percent sure the castle people had not been informed of the evening's true purpose and that these goons had better raise their game and their level of nonchalance if they didn't want to blow their cover. In my humble opinion.

However, the head guy stood at the confluence of hallways, watching me, until I went back through into the Singers' Hall.

"5," I typed, as soon as I was back inside the room. "All armed."

"How many songs left?" he asked.

I moved back to the refreshment table. Matron had

left a program on it, with *Intermission* circled in red after song eight. That was a little odd. Usually intermissions were in the middle, not after song eight of ten. But, I guess, if intermission was your final bidding/purchasing time, you'd only need a couple of songs to process payment and have things sorted out.

"Three songs left before intermission. Then two before the concert ends."

It was helpful being at the back of the room. No one cared about the refreshment guy. They were all really busy with their phones, tablets, and styluses.

There was a momentary pause. Finally, the text response came. "We'd like to get in before intermission, but not sure it can happen. If we can't, we'll wait until intermission is over. We'll let you know when we're coming."

Whew. There. I'd done my thing. I'd gotten them the information they needed. Now I just needed to start pouring red wine and wait for intermission.

Except, of course, you should never think *"Whew."* Ever.

'Cause when I turned back around to see how many more bottles of Riesling I had, I happened to glance up.

It turned out that above the alcove behind me was a

small gallery, where, likely, Ludwig himself planned to sit, away from prying eyes.

A man was sitting up there, in the shadows, even now.

He had been watching me talk to my watch.

Even in the dark, I could tell who it was. Phelan.

We locked eyes.

He was not happy.

CHAPTER TWENTY-NINE

Going Down

WHAT COULD I do? He was watching me. I picked up the box of Riesling and carried it back below him, so he couldn't see me hit the button and hiss, "Phelan's here. And he saw me talk to you. He knows. Get up here *now*."

I turned back, carrying two bottles, trying to act nonchalant. Maybe the long apron fooled him. Maybe he thought I had been planning a date.

On my watch. Yeah, that'll happen.

I glanced back up. He was gone.

I stood by my table, trying my best to see into the

darkness of the alcove. I thought I heard talking, like maybe he was on the steps, talking to the hall guards on his phone.

Or, maybe he was talking to the really, really large bodyguard who had been on the stairs while he was seated above.

The conversation stopped, and the very large clean-shaven man with a buzz cut came lumbering toward me. He was six feet four if he was a day. And built like a boulder. My first thought was that he must have gotten his tux in a "Big and Tall" shop. 'Cause it sure wasn't for sale off the rack. I glanced at my watch, like I was waiting for intermission, and poured a glass of sparkling wine.

As he approached, I smiled and offered it to him. "Champagne?" I asked, and I also offered the full range of food with a sweep of my arm.

This confused him for the slightest second, during which time the girls finished their song. There was scattered applause. The bodyguard stood still next to me while it went on. As the woman directing the singing raised her small baton to begin the next song, I saw her motion to the girls to smile. She didn't need to remind them.

She used a pitch pipe to give them a note, and off

they went on their next song. They were really pretty good. Harmonies swirled and converged.

The bodyguard really wanted to smack that champagne flute out of my hand, but he couldn't do it without calling attention to both of us and making a scene. Before he could decide to simply drag me out back, we both heard a noise, a shuffle from outside in the hallway that became a scuffle. It could be that help was arriving.

Bodyguard turned back around to see Phelan descending the three steps from the alcove. The two of them converged and headed quickly for the small back door.

"Back door. Phelan's heading out into the large hall," I said.

The audience began shuffling, not knowing what was going on or what to do.

The choir members looked confused, but the director was directing, so they kept singing. As the commotion grew louder, the group grew more confused, the song quieter.

My watched buzzed and I read: *Grab the girls and get them out.*

Seriously. Seriously?

Talk about the million-dollar sentence of all time.

There were men's voices, and shouting, from the side hall. The woman director abandoned the concert and ran to the side of the man with the rectangular nose. The audience was shifting, some were standing.

It was now or never.

Domino twenty.

As the confusion heightened, I ran forward, toward the mystified girls. I planted myself right in front of them and said (one guess), "I am a friend of Farrin's. I am here to help. Follow me!" in Pashto.

They stood there, staring. "Follow me!" I said again. Nothing.

A gunshot echoed from the corridor.

"Please!" I said in English. "It isn't safe here!" And, back in Pashto, "Follow me!"

And a tall, slender girl from the back row pushed forward. She spoke quickly, and tersely, to the others. She came up beside me and motioned for me to go.

I hurried down the side aisle, past the outside windows, toward the rear. Everyone's focus seemed, at least momentarily, to be on the side hall and the conflict that was taking place out there. More gunshots exploded. I looked back only once to see if the eleven remaining girls were following.

They were. They had formed a little herd together. They were confused and terrified.

When we got to the back of the darkened room, I paused for them all to arrive, pushed open the wooden door to the corridor, and looked outside.

There were police in uniforms, men in tuxedoes, and others in street clothes, fighting for control of the thinner corridor outside the Singers' Hall. As soon as supremacy was decided, this large hall would be taken over, too.

We had but moments to disappear.

Fortunately, the tower with the small circular staircase was immediately to my left. Its entrance was hidden around the corner; once on the stairs, we would be immediately out of sight.

I motioned the tall girl that way, and she started down, the others behind her. Two girls in the back, who looked younger and more frightened than the others, had started to cry. Which I could fully understand. I got one of the crying girls headed into the staircase; the other stood frozen there, in shock, by the door.

I picked her up. The extra weight on my ankle almost made me scream. I walked into the staircase and put her down and called to the tall girl. I pointed at her two frightened cohorts. She slid sideways, pulled the two stragglers toward her, and began herding them down. Then I realized I couldn't rush down multiple flights of stairs in a floor-length apron, even if I was whole. I stepped back out into the hall to untie it and rip it off—and as I did, my phone came flying out of my pocket and bounced down the hallway. Crap.

It was only two strides away, and so I dove for it.

Domino twenty-one.

As I did, the door across the large hall from the Singers' Hall opened. And out stepped Huge-O, the bodyguard. Double crap.

Had he seen that I had the girls? Had he seen where they had gone?

I made sure not to glance back, in case he hadn't. But now what? If I turned and ran to the stairs, I'd lead him right to them. Even if I could run.

In the instant I was trying to decide what to do, Huge-O was over me. He grabbed me by the arm and hiked it up behind me. Unfortunately, it was my left arm, on my injured side. I yelped in pain.

He pulled me to my feet and told me to walk in some grunt language, but, of course, I couldn't stand on my left foot. So instead he pretty much carried me out of the corridor through the door toward the throne room and kicked the door closed behind us.

He dragged me down a small flight of stairs and dumped me at the bottom.

It took a minute for my eyes to adjust to the lower level of light, which came from the moonlight flowing in through the tall windows across from us. We were in the upper gallery that ran around Ludwig's throne room below. It was quiet and empty. It couldn't be called a gallery, really; there weren't places to sit. In fact, it was barely wide enough to walk around. In the dim light, I saw blue and gold, like the inside of a Byzantine church or a Fabergé egg. A thigh-high wall seemed to run the periphery, with blue pillars holding up golden arches. Real ones.

But there wasn't time to care, because this Phelan guy stood above me. He was no shrinking violet himself. Must have been well over six feet tall—which looked even more menacing from my place on the floor. He didn't work up to threatening me with a gun; it was pointed at my head from the moment Huge-O deposited me on the floor at his boss's feet. The bodyguard stomped back up a couple of steps to watch the scene progress.

"Who are you?" Phelan asked, in German. That much I could understand.

"Gunter," I replied, using up most of my vocabulary in response.

We remained frozen for seconds before he said, in English, "Do you speak English?" He his accent sounded American. Possibly New England.

I nodded weakly. My whole body was shivering in revolt from being dragged and shoved around in its already-battered state. Phelan didn't really have to hold the gun on me. It wasn't like I was going anywhere.

"I don't have much time. Tell me who you are and what's going on. But know this. If you're the catering guy and you know nothing, you're no use to me, so you're dead. If you're some kind of undercover agent and you don't talk, you're no use to me, so you're dead. If you are an agent and you *do* talk, why then, you're of use as a hostage, and your chances of surviving leap to, I don't know, ten percent? So start talking."

I lay there, not knowing what to say. Obviously, I wasn't going to tell him anything. We were a room away from the outside hall, where the action was. But you could hear *something* going on. And every second I didn't say anything, the girls were farther down the stairs.

The girls.

Phelan kicked me, hard, in the ribs on my right side. Which had been, up until now, my uninjured side. I moaned. And it occurred to me that I probably wouldn't live through this encounter.

In my mind, then, I heard my father's voice from my dream, saying that the real way to make girls swoon over you is to get killed on assignment. Preferably saving someone else.

I thought of those eleven girls, hopefully safe, heading down the stairs while I faced down their kidnapper— and the kidnapper of many others. I would die a hero. Like my dad.

Then I thought of my mom, and the pain in her voice as she'd told me the story of the day my dad died. I thought of Victor and Lucy, and how I'd been angry when I left them. How their hearts were already broken, yet healed just enough to be broken again.

I thought of Talya, and how she'd risked her own life to get me here. Although, frankly, it would serve her right if I did get killed. Then, maybe, she'd stop calling me a pre-driver. Maybe she'd even dedicate an album to me.

It's amazing how many things you can think in about half a second.

"Talk, boy. Or do you just want to die?"

Then I realized that, no matter who else thought what, I wanted to live. Me.

Domino twenty-two.

"Hell, no," I roared, and I pulled back my right leg and kicked him hard, with all my might, right in the kneecap. He howled. I rolled. His gun discharged. I didn't see where the bullet went, I only knew it didn't go into me.

As he was cursing, I lurched to my feet and, with all my might, launched into him, knocking him off balance and sending him flying off the balcony, through the archway, to the floor of the throne room below.

He landed with a thud. And a scream.

Huge-O came barreling to look over the railing. He looked terrified. He turned and ran out the way he had come. Was he going down to help his boss? Or making a run for it?

And, if so, would he make a run for it down the turret stairs?

Oh, crap.

I half walked, half crawled back up the throne room stairs. Which made it handy to find my phone where it had fallen on the ground again during my being dragged.

I hit the button, said, "Phelan's injured in the throne

342

room on level three," and headed back out into the hall.

Domino twenty-three.

All hell had broken loose in the corridor behind me. I turned to hobble away from the melee toward the stairs at the other end. As I did, a lone figure came running up into the hall from those stairs. Now what?

I tried to swing back into Gunter mode. As the person approached, I realized it was a female dressed in dark clothing, blonde hair pulled back, weapon drawn, breathing hard.

Familiar. Agent Coltrane.

She had the same moment of startled recognition.

"Who was the big guy who ran past me down the stairs?" she asked.

"Bodyguard," I said.

"Seen Phelan?"

"One floor down. Throne room. Injured."

"You did that?" she asked.

I nodded.

She smiled. Then she turned abruptly and ran back to the stairs.

I followed, more slowly, limping. The turret was small, so the stairs turned severely, and I couldn't see anyone below me. No bodyguard, no agent, no girls.

I hobbled downwards.

I did my best to lean into the interior stone on my right side. There was a maroon velvet rope, and I clung to it, knowing my ankle was going to completely give way at any moment.

I met no one before I reached the third floor. There, one door stood open to the large hall. There was also a small carved door to my right. It was open a crack. As I staggered down, it opened wider. The tall singing girl motioned me in, and quickly shut it behind me.

"Did people come this way?" I asked, and pantomimed a giant coming down the stairs. She nodded and gestured toward the hallway.

Perhaps the best thing now would simply be to get these girls hidden until the bad guys were taken care of. We were in a room that was off of—and open to— the main hall. They were clustered together to hide themselves, but could easily be detected. And there were voices approaching even now. Apparently my message about Phelan had gotten through.

I motioned them to be quiet, and we crept to a closed door across the room, which undoubtedly led deeper into the castle. I opened it enough that they could slip through one at a time. I followed last and shut the door heavily behind me.

We found ourselves in an antechamber. It looked

royal and fancy in the dim light, and we all had the same idea—keep moving, in case someone else decided to open that door.

The next room was Ludwig's dining room. We went through shadowed regality, eerie in the spilled moonlight. At the far end, another carved door. This one led to Ludwig's bedroom. It was a huge, carpeted room, with carved wood paneling all around, crosses at the top of everything, giving it the appearance of a sacristy, one of those rooms at the back of a very old church. Huge painted murals of the story of Tristan and Isolde decorated the top half of the walls. Ludwig's bed was a four-poster with an ornately carved wooden canopy.

Now what? I seemed to remember this was the room where they arrested Ludwig himself. Certainly the girls and I did not want to be stuck here. But, as I recalled the floor plan Talya and I had seen at Robert's, the rooms went in a rectangular pattern. If we kept going through doors, we'd eventually wind up back in the main corridor. That was also no good.

I closed my eyes and tried to remember the floor plan. There should be a little tiny room just off the bedroom. Not the dressing room—that was a large room next door. I led the girls back into the corner, past a large alcove window, and there, as hoped, was another, almost hidden, wooden door.

The room was small and square and looked like a chapel. There were stained glass windows on one wall, and an altar in front. We all barely fit inside. I shut the door.

Once we were in, I tumbled to the floor, head throbbing, not even able to tell where I hurt the most. But I couldn't say anything, because, in the blue stained-glass-filtered moonlight, I saw eleven pairs of eyes, staring at me.

And I knew that I couldn't let one of them panic. Not one. If someone screamed, if someone went running back out into the hall, we were all dead meat.

So I said, in Pashto, "I am a friend of Farrin's. I am here to help."

Ten blank stares. The tall girl gave an irritated sigh. "Would you stop saying that?" she said in English. "Tell me what is going on."

"You speak English?" I said, relieved.

"Yes."

"Only you?"

"The others know some phrases."

So I motioned her to come sit by me. She looked slightly confused, like she wasn't sure what was allowed with a male nonfamily member in a castle oratory in Bavaria. But she did come and sit so we could talk quietly. She said her name was Lida, and, in the absence of AnaSophia, she was the eldest. I told her the story, the short version, as best I could.

As she motioned the other girls around her so she could translate, I fell back against the altar, grateful I didn't have to move again. Hopefully ever.

Which, of course, was the cosmic signal for my watch to buzz.

I hit the button. It was Reese.

"Where are you?" he said.

"Third floor. I've got the girls. They're all safe."

Instead of gratitude, his voice was laced with annoyance and anger.

"Why are you on the third floor?" he asked. "Did I not tell you to get the girls out?"

"You meant out of the *castle*?" I asked.

"What did I tell you about the local authorities? Good people, all. But if they find the girls, they are on the next plane to Kandahar."

No, no, no, no, no. On so many levels, I couldn't be hearing this.

"What am I supposed to do? There's fighting everywhere."

"There's an unmarked white delivery van waiting outside the back door of the old kitchen on the lowest level. You've got approximately three minutes to get those girls on that van before the raid is effectively over and everyone, including our people, will be searching for them."

The old kitchen. Lowest level. Three minutes.

Domino twenty-four. Crap.

CHAPTER THIRTY

Back Door

"LIDA," I SAID, and she looked up at me. "We've got to go."

"What?"

"If we stay here, you will all be sent back to Kandahar. If we can get you down to the lowest level, there is a van that will take you to safety. Where you will be given a good chance, and an education."

Or so I hoped. FALCON wasn't a fairy godmother.

Lida hesitated, like she didn't want the responsibility of deciding what was real and what wasn't. "Please," I said.

I guess I'd been hoping the raid would end and she'd march them off like the von Trapps over the mountains. Instead, it was back to me.

I maneuvered myself to the altar and used my right arm to get to a standing position. "This isn't a joke," I said. "We've got to go right now, or you don't have a chance."

Finally she said, "You're a friend of Farrin's?"

"Yes. She is here—well, near here, anyway. So is AnaSophia. They're safe."

Lida stood processing the information.

"Farrin sent me in to get you to safety."

"She did?"

"Yes. She put herself into great danger to do it."

"If we don't go now, we're sent home?"

"*Right* now." Enough talk. I limped/dragged myself to the door.

Lida again said something short and curt and followed me.

I gave everyone the *shhh* sign, and we plunged through Ludwig's bedroom the same way we'd come. The dining room was also dark and empty, but we lurched through it, and through the antechamber beyond.

Only the reception room was now between us and the hallway where all the action was taking place—and the walls of the reception room were only railing tall.

Lida had apparently had enough of me staggering and waiting. It was she who pulled open the door to the reception room and beckoned the other girls to stay low and be quiet. She pointed them back toward the partially open door to the back stairs. Once she did that, I bit my lip and went first. You never knew who we'd run into. And I had no intention of having them carted off in the wrong van.

Once again in the circular staircase, I again leaned my weight against the interior wall and staggered on my left foot only lightly, while consistently landing heavily on my right.

Neuschwanstein is a very tall castle. Ludwig had only completed the top two floors. The floor underneath was being used as a gift shop and cafeteria. But there were two more unused floors beneath, before we got to the original kitchen and its back door. Which meant three tall floors between us and the door. I reminded myself again of gymnasts who perform at the Olympics on broken legs.

The good thing again was that the circular staircase was in such a confined space that someone looking down wouldn't see us, as soon as everyone had made the first turn.

Except for occasional small lights down by the steps,

the tower was dark. But we all knew what was at stake, and together we soldiered on. And on. And on.

At the final foot of the stairs was a wooden door into a back hallway, which led to the kitchen. I motioned for Lida to stay out of sight and crept forward.

Ludwig's kitchen was large and well lit, with long tables, fireplaces, and huge burnished copper pots. Now there were also two thugs in tuxedoes being arrested by the local police. I had a moment of panic as I wondered if the fact I was wearing a tuxedo might implicate me in the night's proceedings. But I fixed my sights resolutely on the door to the outside and limped straight through. One of the officers looked over at me, but as I reached the final door to outside, a tall man in a white button-down shirt and black trousers came in.

"Looking for a van?" he said to me quietly.

I said yes. He said hurry. As he did, I surreptitiously snapped a photo of him. Back in the hall, I sent it to Reese with the question "Is this our guy?" Reese answered yes.

"Walk quickly," I said to Lida.

She did follow me quickly. The eleven girls, all in bright tunics, pants and chadors, walked in single file through the kitchen, looking straight ahead. The policeman stopped their arrests. The thugs stopped their objecting. They all watched us. Before they could make a move, however, the man in the white shirt gave the officers a small salute, and led us outside.

His quiet calm morphed into a hurried intensity as we approached the unmarked white cargo sprinter van, with no windows except up front. He slid the back door open, and herded the girls in, chanting, "Go. Go. Go."

Then he said to me, "I'm to take you down the mountain. Get in up front."

What sounded simple to him turned out to be, for me, the final million-dollar sentence. The one I couldn't get past. There was a step up. I couldn't coordinate the left half of my body to enter the cab first. I couldn't stand on my left foot to step up with my right. And I definitely couldn't turn enough to make my right arm grasp the seat to pull me in.

White Shirt Guy closed the back slider and came to walk past me. "What's wrong?" he asked. "You took a photo of me. You know I'm the guy."

So he saw me take the picture. How embarrassing. "I can't get in," I said. More embarrassing still.

"Are you hurt?" he asked, and I nodded.

He looked down at my ankle, and even in the dim light it was enough for him to give a surprised gasp. "Just your ankle?" he asked.

I shook my head. "Whole left side. Head. Right ribs."

"I apologize," he said—while he was picking me up and tossing me into the front seat.

I moaned again.

He ran around to the other side, took off the parking break, and headed the van down the mountain.

I sat, gasping and gasping, using every last drop of my strength not to cry. This was not how James Bond ended up. Well, okay, maybe the Daniel Craig versions.

We drove on the narrow winding road that left from the back of the castle, not the wide winding road that led up to the front. Even from a distance, I could see police action up on the other road as we left the castle behind and entered the woods below. The driver was talking, but not to me—to headquarters, I guessed.

He pulled over just before we reached a wider road. Another man was waiting in a dark sedan. The other man opened my side door, and I nearly fell out into his arms.

The van driver didn't say good-bye. As soon as the door was shut, he was gone.

I looked up at the driver of the sedan. Even in the moonlight, there was something familiar about his profile.

"Hey, Colt," he said, "busy day?"

It was Colin. I'd never been so happy to see someone in my life. He wasted no time getting me aboard. Rather than help me limp over to the passenger side, he opened the back door. The sedan had a lower threshold. I got in.

"There's a doctor waiting for you in Munich at one of our facilities. Where is your car?" he asked.

I remembered that the guy whose hang glider we'd taken was going to drive it to Robert's house. "It's at a house here on the lake," I said. "Can we stop there? Please. I need to get my stuff. I need to make sure . . . everything's . . . all right."

"Can you find the house again?" he asked. "Is that where the other girls are?"

Talya Ellis and AnaSophia. The other girls.

"I sure hope so," I said. "Alpseestrasse. It's off Alpseestrasse."

"Okay." He called in this information. "By the way, I said be a bodyguard. Not save the world." I could hear the smile in his voice.

As he drove, I began to relax into the seat. My eyelids were suddenly so very heavy.

Somehow, Colin found Schwan Haus, Robert Rich's mansion. I guess Reese knew the location from before, as they certainly kept track of me on the

GPS. When I opened my eyes, we were in Robert's circular drive and Colin was shaking me gently. "We're here, Colt. We're here. And you can't sleep until we get to Munich. They're afraid you have a concussion."

"How about if I give you two million dollars?" I said. "Could I sleep if I give you two million dollars?" Not that I actually had any money anymore.

He smiled. "Not even then. Sorry, buddy."

Robert came hurrying out to meet us. "Colt!" he said. "Talya's been so worried."

"Talya's here? She's all right?"

"Yes. Got a bit muddy, and slightly bloody, landing in a field or something. But nothing that requires a doctor." He gave me an appraising look. "You, on the other hand . . ."

"I know, I know," I said. "He's taking me to a clinic or something. I just need to get my stuff."

"Well, come on in. Talya should be about out of the shower and dressed."

I let him go ahead into the house. I turned to Colin. "Are we taking Talya Ellis with us? When I landed at the Munich Airport, I was told to get her and take her to a safe house. Also, the girl AnaSophia is here."

"Someone is being sent to bring them in safely and

debrief them. Hear their side of the story, what they know that can help," he said. "But they're civilians. They'll be on a different track. Whereas you're mine. It's my job to get you to the doc as soon as possible."

We had walked into the entrance/ballroom. The dapper Brit didn't even react to the splendor around him.

"Talya said she was starving. Judy is setting dinner for us and AnaSophia even now. Can you eat, at least?" Robert asked from the balcony that ringed the entrance hall.

I remembered the cheese sticks and how famished I was. I looked hopefully at Colin. He shook his head. "No sleep until they're sure you don't have a concussion, and no food until we're sure you don't need surgery."

"Next time, remind me to read the fine print," I said.

"Talya's almost ready," said Robert. "Why don't you go on up?" Then, seeing the look on my face, "Use the elevator."

Of course he had an elevator.

I waited for Talya on the rounded outside balcony on the second story of Schwan Haus.

"It all looks so peaceful and lovely and innocent, doesn't it?" she asked. I turned as she came out. She beckoned past me to the lake, Alpsee, dark and shimmering, the reflection of the nearly full moon mirrored in the water below, with the fairy tale castle perched in the distance. The scene was impossibly perfect. A picture from a postcard or a wall poster.

"Robert says you're injured. Is it bad?"

"I don't know," I said. "I'm still standing. He said you had a rough landing."

"Got some scrapes from a tree on the way down, but nothing that won't heal by next week. Don't change the subject. What happened to you?"

"Hard landing at Neuschwanstein," I said. "Then getting picked up and dumped various places, and finally kicked in the ribs."

"The girls?" she asked.

"I am a friend of Farrin's," I said, and smiled. "It sort of worked. Until Lida told me to speak English."

"Lida speaks English?"

"Yes."

"And they're safe?"

"Yes."

"Where are they being taken?"

"I don't know."

"But you trust FALCON."

"Yes. So does your mother."

"I know you're in pain," she said, "and I don't want

to keep you. Is there any way I can give you a hug that won't hurt?"

No, was the actual answer. Absolutely not. But I opened my right arm and pulled her to me. She turned to face me. "Will you promise, as soon as this is all over, to tell me everything that happened?"

I nodded. "You too."

Talya Ellis looked up at me. I realized how the face before me had gone from being that of a stranger to someone I trusted most in the whole world. She looked in my eyes. Then, overlooking the lake and the moon and the castle, with the autumn leaves rustling, she stood on tiptoe. And she kissed me. It wasn't a sisterly peck. It was a real, serious kiss. Somehow, for the space of that one minute, I forgot everything that hurt. I forgot everything mean she'd ever said. I forgot everything except her.

Dominos twenty-five through twenty-nine. The Empire State Building.

Then Colin coughed from the background. We pulled apart.

"Bye, Spy Guy," she said.

I didn't answer. I didn't know what to say.

Front Door

THAT'S HOW MY first assignment ended.

I was in a safe-house/clinic in Munich for three days. My ribs were bruised and I did have a slight concussion. My ankle was severely sprained, which I was told would take longer to heal than a break. I had bruises and contusions all up my left side, which was less serious than, but hurt more than, almost anything else. Nothing for it but time. Colin stopped in a couple times, and it was great to see him. I was sorry he couldn't always be my tether.

From Munich I flew back to the United States and

stayed with my mom near Chicago for a week while Dr. Verhagen oversaw my recuperation. Mr. Waverly thought giving my mother the time off was the least he could do. We had a good time, the two of us sitting on the sofa, eating popcorn and watching movies.

Of course, we also talked about Phelan. She told me about other terrible things he'd done and how she'd figured out who he was. She asked to hear the story about me sending him sailing down to Ludwig's throne room floor about seventeen times.

As I felt better, we went to the Brookfield Zoo and the Museum of Science and Industry. It felt like making up for childhood time we hadn't gotten to share. I came to understand how she felt letting Lucy and Victor raise me was the best thing. Even though I never could bring myself to say so, I began to suspect the same thing.

Colin didn't finish his part of the assignment until I was almost well enough to go back to Springfield. He joined us for dinner the night before I flew home.

I did end up talking with a therapist once I was back in Springfield, as Amber suggested during our first meeting, because every active agent is assigned someone with whom we can talk candidly about stuff like who we killed or didn't kill, and how we feel about it. (Fortunately, I didn't kill anybody. Both Hoth, the guy at Eagle's Nest, and Mr. Phelan were apprehended worse for the wear but not permanently damaged.) I admit it's good to have somebody I can talk to about my family situation and who treats crazy assignment stuff like it's normal.

Back at school, I was switched onto not only a "future operative" track, but also a "working operative" track. Luke was still my best friend; likely he always will be. I chose him as the one person Colin recommended I have with whom I can share anything.

However, I also started hanging out with Jonathan Kryder sometimes. (And I found out he prefers "Jonathan" to "Jonny Baad." Big surprise there.) We started hanging out naturally because we have some classes together and because he also plays the drums. I soon found he wasn't that gregarious with the other kids, not because he was stuck up, but because, well, not everyone understands that sometimes being an operative hurts. A lot. And you have to deal with people and situations that aren't nice. Things are often ambiguous. Sometimes the people you're saving don't want to come. They cry in the backseat.

Also, your priorities tend to shift when you face your own death—and then say, sure, I'll do it again.

So, when the other kids at school smile and high-five

you and think you're cool, that's nice. But it sure isn't the whole story.

I also started dating Malin James, the girl I thought hadn't noticed me. The girl I was afraid to talk to. One good thing about being forced to hold your own with someone like Talya Ellis is that talking to other girls—heck, talking to any normal human being—suddenly becomes much easier. It turned out that Malin had noticed me after all, which might be one reason I'd thought she was nice.

She was.

She is.

Malin comes over a lot after school to do homework and listen to me play the drums. She plays keyboards. She's pretty good. Not rock-star good, but, really, who is?

Rhetorical question.

Talya and I didn't get to keep our promise to tell each other the rest of the story of our night. While I was whisked away to secure FALCON places to recover, Talya joined Thorne again, safely back in the States, and Shadow started a big tour. With Rip Ettinger, one of the best drummers in the world, on whom I'd heard Talya was crushing.

One nice thing was that both AnaSophia and Lida started attending our school. I would have been happy to welcome them and show them around, but it was clear that having a coed student body was enough of a challenge for them. They made friends first with some of the girls who were Muslim, who welcomed them and showed them the ropes. Eventually, slowly, they began to branch out. They were in the think-tank track, and I'm sure their background and experiences brought a lot to the discussions. One of their friends told me the other girls from Afghanistan had been placed safely with families and schools in cultures that felt more familiar to them.

As time went on, sometimes when I passed Lida or AnaSophia in the hallway, they'd give me a shy smile, which was all the thanks I needed.

Things changed at home too. First, I apologized to Lucy and Victor for how I'd acted when I was so angry. They apologized for keeping my true parentage a secret. I still wish they hadn't. Or that I hadn't been blindsided by the truth when it finally came out.

Maybe the biggest change is the smallest thing. I now often come in through the front door. I give Dix's photo a little salute as I do. There are things that only the two of us share, that only the two of us understand.

For one thing, we're proud of each other. I know that for a fact.

Here's the other crazy thing. These days, I carry a smooth mini-domino in my pocket. Just to remind me that a normal day might not turn out to be so normal after all.

I think Dix would understand that as well.

ACKNOWLEDGEMENTS

Thanks to my young FALCONers, Cleveland Benedict, Tyler Best, Sam Caldwell, Nate Love, Erin Eileen Shanahan, Ryan Robert Stiskin, and Hannah Tucker, who are still there, know what it's like, and whose suggestions were critical to the completion of the story. Thanks also to Mark, Ken, and Gary, the car guy, the fly guy, and the spy guy.

ABOUT THE AUTHOR

Axel Avian grew up in an organization not unlike FALCON in a town not unlike Springfield, Missouri. He has traveled the world for his work. To relax, he enjoys sky and scuba diving, hang gliding, rock climbing, and snowboarding. He speaks four languages, reads whenever he can, and routinely trounces opponents on video games. (Bring it.) He would also like to note that he is humble, easily amused, and occasionally very funny.

If you liked Colt Shore try
The Wacko Academy Series,
written by Moonbeam Award
winning teen author Faith Wilkins.
Available wherever books are sold.

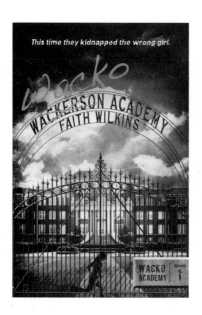

Prologue to *Wacko Academy*

I stared out the window, head swimming from the height. The voices from behind me had grown louder, angrier. There wasn't much time left. I had to jump now. My friend's life depended on it. Heck, my life depended on it, but fear seemed to have frozen every muscle in my body. I was completely immobilized.

The others stared up at me, wondering why I hadn't done anything yet. I was holding them all up, compromising everything. Maybe they would have to leave me. No, I couldn't let that happen. This was my only chance. Footsteps joined the voices now. I closed my eyes, wondering how it could have come to this . . .

The *Now* You Tell Me! Series
Fun, fast and unforgettable.

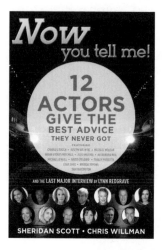

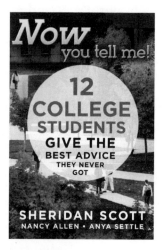

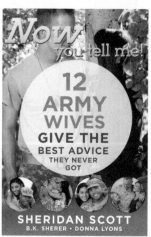

The inside information
that no one should be without.
www.nowyoutellmebooks.com
Available wherever books are sold.